# BURIED ALIVE!

Suddenly enveloped in the complete darkness of the root cellar, Roy heard a deadbolt lock slammed home over his head. He looked around, or tried to. Whether he turned his head left or right, up or down, he saw nothing, not a timber, or even his own hand held inches in front of his face.

He knew one thing without benefit of vision. The air was dead. He reached out, fingertips touching dirt walls and rough-cut timbers, and wondered how long it would take to suffocate in here...

# STEPHEN OVERHOLSER

## WEST OF THE MOON

LEISURE BOOKS  NEW YORK CITY

A LEISURE BOOK ®

January 2005

Published by special arrangement with Golden West Literary Agency.

Dorchester Publishing Co., Inc.
200 Madison Avenue
New York, NY 10016

ISBN 0-8439-5485-X

The name "Leisure Books" and the stylized "L" with design are trademarks of Dorchester Publishing Co., Inc.

Printed in the United States of America.

Visit us on the web at www.dorchesterpub.com.

# Prologue

Lying prone on matted leaves and tangled twigs, the scout fought off sleep. He drank from his canteen and sloshed water over his face. Resting for as long as he dared, he struggled to keep his eyes open. Then he pressed on, Springfield at the ready as he belly-crawled through the layered compost of countless autumns in a forest unknown to him.

He halted when a distant roar reached his ears. It grew louder. The sound of a storm drew his gaze skyward where he beheld an odd sight. Overhead in the treetops wind-whipped branches bent double, twigs snapped free, and leaves pulled loose—all of the débris swirling upward to be carried away. Yet at ground level the air was still, the forest quiet as a tomb. It was strange, he thought, this quietude directly under a raging windstorm.

While he watched the phenomenon, a premonition came to him. He did not know what the future held, if he would survive the hour much less the day, but he sensed this moment was etched into his memory. Somehow he knew this fragment of time would stay with him to the end. What it meant, beyond a random event captured in his mind, he did not know. Not then. Only later would he learn these were the final hours of the war, that nothing of the old was left in the new.

*Whump! Whump! Whump!*

The heavy rumble of a cannonade shook the ground. He figured Reb 12-pounders had found the range. If so, enemy infantry would soon charge Fox Run where his company was dug in. Eighty-four riflemen of the 112th New York were left. Among them a dozen or fifteen were wounded. Most of the command suffered from dysentery. Bandaged or not, lying in watery feces or not, they waited with bayonets fixed, muddy and bloody and blue, all of them under the dreaded order: Hold the position. The scout had been sent out at dawn with orders to locate Rebs on their left. How many? How close? On the move? These were questions he must answer before returning to Fox Run.

The storm passed, and the roar dwindled to a distant shout shredded to whispers in the boughs. A moment later the scout felt a presence. Obeying instinct over reason, he did not move. Whether he had caught scent or sound he did not know. Presently the muffled beat of shod hoofs reached him—one horse, unseen.

The scout peered through the trees. He watched a rider approach at a walk, slowly and ghost-like, no more than thirty yards away. From his prone position he saw a gray trouser leg, the lower hem of a gray tunic edged in black, and a red sash tied to the handle of a saber. It was the uniform of a Confederate officer, the sash undoubtedly a remembrance from his wife or betrothed. Now the Reb angled away in a clearing, close enough for the scout to hear a creak of saddle leather. Close enough to kill him.

He raised up on his elbows. Cocking the hammer of his rifled musket, he pressed the butt plate to his shoulder and raised the barrel. He aligned front and rear sights and drew aim just as the rider halted. Index finger inside the trigger guard now, he aimed dead center between the man's shoulder blades.

The moment passed. He lowered the musket. Holding the hammer with his thumb, he squeezed the trigger and eased the hammer down. He looked past the gunsights at the rider.

The report of a firearm here would alert Reb skirmishers. Common sense. Still, it was a strange sensation to let a big fish go. That uniform was as clean as new, an indication of high rank in the eyes of an enlisted man.

As a veteran of hundreds of skirmishes and half a dozen full-scale battles, the scout might well have killed or wounded dozens of men from his position on the firing line. Or more. He did not know. He would never know. But just now he had held a man's life in his hands, one trigger pull away from the Great Beyond. Watching the rider pick his way through the forest to live another day, or instant, was one more image fixed in his mind this day.

Treetops stilled now, the branches cut sharp, angular shadows on the forest floor. Quietude again settled over him. The vast silence was a weight that seemed to push downward, pressing him into decayed matter as though the specter of death was here. Then he glimpsed movement through the trees to his right.

Swinging the barrel of his musket around, the scout turned to meet his fate. Another Reb, he figured. Maybe a squad. If caught here, he was dead. How many men he would take with him was the only question in his mind as he stared into the forest. That was when he saw the creature.

Man or beast, he did not know in that first moment. What he saw defied easy description. Bent low, two legged, long, black hair, skinny arms pumping—the creature dashed into dense undergrowth. As any hunter knows, one spooked animal signifies hot pursuit by a predator. Deciding this was not the place where he would die, the scout scrambled to his feet.

Springfield in hand, he sprinted to the gap in the woods where he had last seen the creature. Bulling his way through branches, he moved as fast as he could, clumsy and noisy with the effort. He burst into a meadow, and halted. Before him, a vegetable patch grew around the perimeter of a bog, the peat bearing a sheen where water seeped to the surface. In soft ground, he saw tracks—small bare feet, human.

Edging around the bog, he made his way through the meadow, slower now, and quieter. An escarpment swelled up before him. At its base lay a shadow. Moving closer, the scout halted. The crescent-shaped shadow was the mouth of a cave. It was not deep enough to conceal the naked creature kneeling in there, a human figure cornered and trembling, watching him.

Dropping to a knee, the scout peered under this massive granite uplift. In the cave, charred sticks marked a fire pit. Rabbit and squirrel skulls and gnawed bones were scattered on the ground amid tufts of fur.

From the back of the cave dark eyes peered at him, a small face under matted black hair, shoulder-length. The creature clutched an article of clothing, butternut in color. The scout recognized it. Reb officers wore gray, but, with fabric in short supply, common soldiers were now issued thin uniforms dyed brown, the color extracted from crushed walnut shells.

This was no soldier. Even in dim light the scout saw a bullet hole in the fabric, a hole encircled by a dark bloodstain. The scout figured that garment had been stolen by the creature, pulled from a corpse on a battlefield or the site of an ambush.

Man or woman? Young or old? White? Black? Red? Yellow? The scout did not know skin color or other means of identification. The thought crossed his mind that he had stumbled upon a member of a lost tribe. Such tales abounded in periodicals, melodramas portraying a remnant of some fictitious culture decimated after a clash with brutal invaders. Other yarns claimed the Lost Tribe of Israel existed in remote reaches of North America.

The creature edged out of the cave—eyes fixed on the scout—bolted—disappeared in undergrowth and a maze of forest shadows.

The scout moved closer to the cave. He peered in. The inhabitant must have been part pack rat. The cave floor was littered with brass buttons, corroded shell casings, a battered Union kepi, a rusted folding knife, a musket ramrod, one slender book.

The scout reached down and picked up the book. He held it to the light. Water-damaged and warped, the title was dim but readable—*West of the Moon*. He opened it to find a volume of verse on wrinkled pages. The flyleaf was inscribed in a feminine hand, but moisture had bled away the inked lettering. *Love forever* were the only words he could decipher above a blurred signature. He tossed the book back into the cave. It flipped over on its back and came to rest with the other spoils of war.

Backtracking, the scout left the bog and garden patch in the lush meadow. He eased out of the dense undergrowth near the spot where he had lain when the mounted Confederate officer passed by. Now he heard the whicker of another horse.

The scout dropped down. Listening intently, he inched forward. He moved slowly until he came in sight of the clearing. He stopped then, wondering if this rider had flushed the creature from hiding.

Sitting his horse, the Reb was readily identified by the red sash tied to his saber handle. With no junior officers or infantry in sight, it was clear he was alone. Alone and waiting. When he turned in the saddle, the scout saw a pair of stars sewn to the shoulders of his uniform. Those squared shoulders under a clean tunic and the set of his clean-shaven jaw lent him a certain demeanor, a pose. The language of his posture suggested a man of privilege, an aristocrat in uniform.

The horse snorted, head bobbing. The Reb reined him down. Presently another rider entered the clearing—a brigadier general in Union blue. He greeted the Reb as he reined up. The two men reached across their saddles to shake hands.

Shocked by the unbelievable sight, the scout lay as still as stone. He heard voices, not words. The two generals spoke congenially, their manner easy.

The scout's mind raced. For weeks rumors had circulated as though blown by winds. He wondered—had the Reb command buckled? Judging by the relaxed manner of these two opposing officers, they were neither sworn enemies demanding surrender nor one jubilant West Pointer proclaiming victory over the other.

Full-bearded and stout as a barrel, the Union general wore a standard-issue campaign hat with a plume. The scout had never seen him before. In fact, this was the closest he had ever been to any general, Union or Confederate. He thought about that as he stared at the two supposed enemies.

During three years and seven months of serving nine regiments in front line reconnaissance, he had scouted terrain bearing names foreign to his ear—Manassas, Fredericksburg, Chickamagua, Kennesaw Mountain—and in all of these marches he had seen but one general. That anonymous commander had stood at attention during review after the battle at Chancellorsville in May of 1863. His salute frozen in place, he had stared at the horizon while soldiers passed by in formation. If that general had been carried off later as a piece of statuary, the scout would not have been surprised.

Now he watched these two generals dismount. They shared a pint, talked in low tones, laughed softly, and tossed the bottle aside. Working together, they pulled weighty saddlebags off the Reb's horse. They carried them to the Union general's mount and secured them behind his saddle. After a parting handshake, the men swung up, turned their horses, and went their separate ways.

The scout raised up. He stared after them as though an explanation lingered in the shadows of a forest once again silent as a crypt. At last he got to his feet. He turned and backtracked 600 yards. Dropping down, he belly-crawled through the underbrush as he inched his way toward Fox Run. A familiar stone footbridge came into view. No pickets challenged him.

Stopping, he looked ahead. Colors were down. He raised up and advanced, Springfield cocked. Scattered clods of mud and depressions showed where the earth had been cratered by artillery rounds. The sight of the damaged footbridge brought him to a scene of carnage. Bodies lay sprawled on the muddy banks of Fox Run.

The scout walked along a churned bank to the bridge. He saw the bodies of eighty-four Union soldiers, eighty-four men smashed, bloodied, dismembered. Raw flesh was pierced by jagged white bones. Blood pooled, dark as mud. The men of the 112th New York lay in the terrible and awkward poses of death, some open-eyed. A few had crawled a short distance before dying.

Tears came, but this was not the time for the abandon of sobbing grief. The scout jogged across the footbridge. He hurried along the grassy bank, bound for regimental headquarters some two miles distant. He had covered a few hundred yards when forest shadows moved on his left. He halted and half turned, raising his Springfield.

Shaggy men in mismatched butternut and gray uniforms stepped out of the trees. The line of Reb infantry numbered twenty riflemen or more, a squad backed up by still more men emerging from the dark forest. Swift strides across open ground marked them as veterans. Their sergeant hefted his musket.

"Slant yer gun down, Blue-Belly. Slant her down 'less ye aim be the last damned fool kilt in this-here war."

The scout lowered his Springfield, a gesture that was an act of courtesy, not surrender by a Federal to the Rebels. For he sensed no danger here, not even with the enemy closing in, not even with the corpses of eighty-four good men lying in their blood behind him.

The Rebs looked tired, he thought, seeing hollow-eyed faces unshaven, dirty. He recognized empty stares and slouched shoulders. Worn-out and plumb fought out, every man among them was resigned to his fate, whatever it was.

"Ain't ye heard?" a second Reb demanded.

Another spoke up: "The war's over, ye stinkin' Yankee."

"Go home," said another.

"Burn in hell," shouted a fourth man.

The sergeant thrust out his musket. "Go on, git!"

The scout stared at the ragged line of Confederate soldiers, the last he would ever see.

"Git!" the sergeant shouted again. "Git outta Virginny!"

# Chapter One

"Progress, hell. Steel rails are ramming civilization down our throats. Straight down our throats. That's progress for you, Royal."

On the L-Bar-7 Ranch, Roy Smith listened to his uncle hold forth. Every other Saturday morning he was a captive audience in his own house. Uncle Ab was a talker, a spouter of opinions, a debater dead certain of his pronouncements and prophesies. Ab's rigidly held views seemed unassailable, the final word, until Roy had time to think things over and separate blue sky exaggerations from bedrock truth.

One thing was certain. There was no arguing with the man, even if Roy wanted to, which he did not. Arguing only fueled the fire. Besides, by the time Roy lined up his should-have-saids, Uncle Abner was off bushwhacking new trails for another one-sided debate, loudly formulating opinions on the next subject to catch his eye and stir his wrath.

"This wild land was meant for men and critters, Royal. Far as the eye can see, critters roam. Elk or deer, antelope or buffalo, four-legged critters on this land have been trailed by men afoot or astride a horse. The buffalo are gone, pushed out by rail and by fence. Gone in the name of progress. We're all gonna choke on dust raised by 'civilization'. You'll see, Royal."

Roy saw his uncle draw a ragged breath. The man's face was deeply lined and leathery, his pale gaze stern as a hawk's.

"Too damned many nesters, Royal. They're plowing too much land and fencing off too many water holes. Cowmen

15

are cutting fence lines, pulling posts, and using cattle to trample sodbuster crops. By damn, we're headed for revolution. Another damned war, that's what we'll have. You ready to fight again?"

Bombastic and prone to exaggeration as he was, in some measure Abner's views were prophetic. The UP laid steel into Colorado, the tracks dropping down from Laramie where the main Union Pacific east-west line sliced through southern Wyoming. With that spur came printing presses, farriers' anvils and blacksmith's bellows, and saloon backbars with full-size diamond dust mirrors. A horse-drawn water wagon and road grader delivered on flat cars to the town of Hat Creek brought one triumphant message—civilization had arrived.

The sawmill sang as steam-powered machinery went into operation on the bank of the creek. Hand-hewn logs of the pioneer era were replaced by pine boards. Lumber was ripped, boards crosscut to standard dimensions, and the wood dried under the Colorado sun to limit warping. In town, new stores and modest houses were built on the prairie by squads of carpenters.

Settlers arrived by train car and by wagon. Boxcars brought an array of tools and gear, spools of wire and kegs of nails, men's and ladies' clothing, all manner of household furnishings, paint and whitewash, chairs, settees, rolls of wallpaper, pianos, books, oil lamps, bolts of fabric, high-button shoes, notions. From wheat flour to sardines, a steady stream of barrels and packing crates brought foodstuff from warehouses east of the Missouri.

"Sky-high prices and fat-assed merchants," Ab complained about goods from Benson's Mercantile. "There's your progress, Royal."

In cattle country of the 1880s, one-room, dirt-floored log cabins were torn down or relegated to the status of outbuildings. The low, sod-roofed structures fashioned by pioneers were replaced by fine ranch houses with peaked roofs of pine shakes, gingerbread trim, and shaded verandahs. Two-story homes took shape with casement windows and real doors sporting cut-glass panels. Those doors were hung on machined hinges instead of cowhide straps holding a plank door in the frame of a log cabin.

Ab Smith was not the only one to object to a plague named "civilization" and the attendant disease known as "progress". The survival of large ranches requiring open range was pressured as never before. Old-timers longed for bygone times, an era when die-outs of winter and starve-outs of summer represented the greatest dangers to their herds. Ranchers figured a man had a fighting chance against seasonal enemies. But a homesteader from afar laying claim to water holes was an adversary no one had yet defeated.

In retaliation, established ranchers hogged more and more open range. A common practice was to turn herds loose in the swells and valleys of the high plains, those endless miles of rolling grasslands stretching across northern Colorado into the far reaches of Wyoming. If a settler's garden plot happened to get trampled, cowhands took no notice. If nester cattle got mixed in with the herd, so much the better. The running iron stowed in a cowhand's saddlebag was handy for branding mavericks on the open range—and altering brands not listed in the *Cattleman's Brand Bo*ok.

Ranchers formed stock growers' associations to combat the threat presented by "our mighty infestation of nesters, locusts, and prairie rats", as first reported in the Cheyenne "Cattleman" *Leader* and later disputed by the editor of the Laramie "Live and Let Live" *Boomerang*. Meeting periodically in Cheyenne, these ranchers drank shots of Kentucky bourbon and shrewdly eyed smoke trailing from their Cubans. Cuss-and-discuss was the order of the day as they tried to figure out how in hell to turn back the tide.

Conflicts erupted. Some disputes amounted to no more than barroom fist fights. At times, though, gunfire was exchanged as one side or the other defended their God-given "right". In the cattlemen's parlance, this right was anchored to one overriding principle, a time-honored tradition in the West: I was here first, you son-of-a-bitch. Unrecognized by the lower courts, that particular "right" to open range lands had never made it past preliminary hearings.

The UP railroad spur gave residents of Hat Creek access to newspapers published in the region. Roy read them all, old and new. He did not know how the rancher-homesteader dispute would all come out. For himself, his L-Bar-7 was too small to be considered a threat to the big boys, too large to be aligned with homesteaders.

The whole deal was a losing battle for both sides, he figured. The big ranchers must have sensed it all went for naught. Their meetings, their arguments, their threats—none of it changed the basic fact of life in cattle country. Settlers were coming, more every spring and summer.

On this sunny Saturday morning, Roy handed Uncle Ab a shopping list and watched him drive away in his buckboard wagon. Ab had come from his own ranch, the Box R, and crossed L-Bar-7 range to his nephew's front porch. Headed for the town of Hat Creek, Ab stopped here every other Saturday to pick up Roy's list and letters home.

Uncle and nephew, Ab and Roy were neighbors by design. After mustering out of the Army in the spring of 1865, Roy had worked the Smith family's farm and tended their dairy herd in Waterville, Maine. He read and re-read Uncle Ab's letters. He imagined wide-open spaces as he labored behind the plow in Maine, daydreaming while avoiding exposed boulders. He often wrote to Ab, expressing his yearning to see the West.

Roy had decided he did not want to plant, harvest, clear ditches, milk cows, and separate cream for the rest of his days. Yet he saw no viable alternative, not until word came from Uncle Ab that a neighboring ranch in Colorado was available for back taxes. Ab urged purchase of the L-Bar-7, quick, before word spread and someone else came up with the cash.

*Send Royal. Send him if you don't want to miss out on owning the finest spread this side of the Platte.*

Roy was the one who did not want to miss out. His father and his two younger brothers and their sister could manage the family farm without him. This letter from Uncle Ab marked the opportunity of a lifetime. Somehow, some way, Roy was determined to take it.

A long line of Mainers, Albert was Abner's older brother. By far the more conservative of the two, Albert had settled in Waterville and married, siring four children. Ab was the life-long bachelor of the Smith tribe, an adventurer who had traveled out West long before war broke out between the States.

*The American West is Paradise for a man strong enough and savvy enough to survive,* Ab once wrote. *This here is a land of endless beauty with natural treasures just a-waitin' discovery.*

Albert knew Ab was partial to Roy for he never failed to inquire about him in letters. Now, after some persuasion, brother Al co-signed a loan agreement with the bank. Lock, saddle stock, and barrel, Roy bought the L-Bar-7 sight unseen with his family's backing. Joining a wagon caravan of settlers, he journeyed West.

Roy was relieved to discover Ab had not exaggerated, at least not beyond all reason. His father had cautioned him about that trait. Brother Ab was known to embroider as he spun a yarn.

On that first day after Roy's arrival, Uncle Ab presented an L-Bar-7 branding iron to him as a welcoming gesture. Turning it, he pointed out a novelty. The brand read the same way right side up as it did upside down.

Ab took him for a ride along property lines. Grasslands stretched through a series of shallow valleys and low hills on the upper reaches of Hat Creek Basin. A tributary to the Platte, this creek meandered through lush grass to the town bearing the same name.

While the L-Bar-7 was several steps short of paradise, it was a fine cattle and horse property with bluestem, grama, and other native grasses, all of them flourishing in winter-sheltered range.

In addition to the creek, the property was marked by spring-fed water holes and buffalo wallows. Ab pointed to flint spear points and feathered arrow shafts scattered on the ground near the dusty wallows. Hunter and prey were long gone, he said, with native people and wild beasts no longer roaming their homelands to migrate with the seasons.

From displaced Mainer to a Westerner at home on the Colorado range, Roy adapted to his new life. He had never worked so hard nor had he ever drawn such satisfaction from his labors. For the most part he was a man alone, a man on horseback riding a vast plain to tend livestock and nurse steers—nurse them through weather extremes of howling winter blizzards and blistering summer heat waves. Roy rode his range in all seasons, often taking time out to lend a hand to his uncle.

At first appearances, Ab looked as sturdy as his opinions. But Roy was aware time was a race won by no man, and he could see the toll of years slowing his uncle. For strenuous work Ab needed help. Come spring and fall roundups, uncle and nephew worked side-by-side to gather and brand critters. In the autumn, triple-wintered steers were driven to the loading pens at Hat Creek for shipment by rail to Laramie and on to the Chicago stockyards for slaughter.

Despite the relentless march of civilization, Ab grudgingly admitted business had never been better, beef prices in Chicago never higher. Roy cheered to the heavens when cash on the hoof brought that most memorable day to anyone who had ever shouldered a debt—his final payment to the bank in Waterville. Even better, he started a savings account at the Laramie Trust. Across the state line in Wyoming, it was the nearest bank.

Roy could just about set his wind-up eight-day clock by Uncle Ab. Weather permitting, the man's routine every other Saturday was to head for town to bathe and shave in the tonsorial parlor. After staying overnight in the Plainsman Hotel, he would return Sunday with a whiskey headache, a stack of Colorado and Wyoming newspapers, and a wagonload of goods from the mercantile.

Sometimes Roy made the three-hour trip with him, but more often he stayed on the home place. When it came to the gift of gab, he was the polar opposite from his uncle. Ab took pride in his talent for elocution, and relished bar-pounding saloon debates on subjects ranging from politics to religion to horses. Whether half drunk or fully hammered, when the shouting was done, he invariably lifted his shot glass to proclaim victory.

Roy knew Ab did not take the hollering matches seriously, mere sport, and volatile subjects igniting disputes were lost in a fog of hangovers the next morning. Not so for Roy. Barroom arguments left him stirred up for days. Solitude on the ranch suited him.

Roy was expecting Uncle Ab to return from town when he

heard the rattling wagon and a booming voice.

"Hello, the house!"

He came out on the verandah, surprised by the sight before him. Following Ab's buckboard was a surrey. The vehicle was pulled by a team of speckled gray geldings, an outfit Roy recognized from the Hat Creek Livery. A man and woman were seated on the leather-tufted bench seat with two young children in the seat behind them. All of them wore long dusters, neckerchiefs, and hats.

"Royal!" Ab said, hauling back on the reins. "This-here gent's been a-hunting you."

"Me," Roy said.

"He won't tell me what for," Ab said. "Says he'll talk to Private Royal Smith of the Hundred and Twelfth New York, and nobody else."

Roy shifted his gaze to the visitors. The man set the brake and took off his hat. They eyed one another. Red-haired and clean-shaven, he was double-chinned with dark eyes nearly buried in folds of flesh.

The woman at his side was handsome, with full lips, a slender nose, and prominent cheek bones. Flaxen hair was pinned up under a wide-brimmed straw hat. Her eyes lingered on Roy until the children spoke up behind her.

"Can we? Can we?"

"With the rancher's permission," the woman said after a glance back at them. "Mister Smith, I'd like you to meet our son and daughter, William and Henrietta. They wish to wade in your creek."

Roy's gaze met her brown eyes again. The two children let out a cheer when he nodded. They leaped from the surrey, shedding dusters and shoes. Roy knew nothing of children, but guessed their ages to be eight and ten or so, the girl being the oldest.

They ran past the pole corral and barn to the bank of Hat Creek. Even in springtime the creek was shallow, curving into a sandy bank as it flowed toward town.

The man climbed out of the surrey and handed the woman down. Unbuttoning their dusters, they took them off and draped them across the seat of the vehicle. Then the man turned to Roy.

"Name's John Nichols," he said, blinking against the bright afternoon sun. "This is my wife, Anne."

"Mister Smith," she said, "I am pleased to make your acquaintance."

Roy watched her reach up behind her head. Pulling out a long hatpin, she took off her hat and gently placed it on her canvas duster, and turned to him. She smiled.

"Likewise," Roy said, suddenly uncomfortable as he wondered if he had somehow violated proper manners. He figured he had stared, and long ago his mother had told him staring was impolite. Roy thought about that, just now realizing visitors had never come to his ranch before, expected or unexpected, in all these years. Alone here with no one but Uncle Ab for company, he was uncertain of correct behavior in the presence of guests.

"We've come a long way, Mister Smith," Nichols said.

"You seem to have the edge on me," Roy said as he stepped down from the porch. Polite or not, he asked a pointed question: "Have we met somewhere?"

"Formally, no," Nichols said. "But I must say, I feel like I know you. I have been searching for you for the better part of four years."

"Four years!" Ab exclaimed.

"Mister," Roy said, "you have somebody else in mind."

Ab laughed. "That's what I told him. These folks don't even hail from Maine. They're from New York!"

"Albany," Nichols said, adding: "A fact that explains why it took me so long to find you."

Roy asked: "How's that?"

"At war's end, you were serving with the One Hundred and Twelfth New York," he said. "I assumed you to be a New Yorker. A logical conclusion, wouldn't you say? I searched my home state up and down, looking for you."

Still mystified, Roy asked: "Why?"

"If I may have a few minutes of your time," he answered, "I shall explain everything."

Roy studied him. Then he caught the hint. He motioned to his door. "Reckon we ought to get out of the sun while we figure this thing out."

Ab stepped down from the buckboard wagon. In stiff-legged strides, he mounted the steps and led the way across the verandah to the front door. "Come in, folks, come in. I'll brew a pot of coffee while you're jawing with my nephew."

Roy followed, grateful Ab had horned in and taken charge. Roy was content to bring up the rear. He felt self-conscious when he cleared the doorway and saw Anne Nichols looking around at the interior of his small ranch house, her eyes bright with curiosity. Over the years he had made a few improvements, but not many.

Dimly lit by four windows, the place was Spartan and odorous, a man's domain with a lever-action Winchester mounted on elk antlers over the hearth of a stone fireplace. Bear-hides covered a plank floor. The kitchen area was defined by a woodstove, a stack of firewood, paper, and the ever-present buckets for lugging water from the creek. On the wall open shelves held tins and jars. Nearby, a plank table was flanked by two benches. Across the room a threadbare quilt from home hung from the ceiling to partition the bunk.

"Have a seat, folks," Ab said over his shoulder as he

crossed the room to the kitchen. With a loud clatter, he lifted a stove lid and stoked the fire. After the guests were seated at the table, Roy pulled up a stool. He sat down and faced Nichols.

"Now, Mister Smith," Nichols said, "I am a historian by training. Presently I am compiling information for a history of the Hundred and Twelfth New York, a regiment of heroes. You, sir, are the mysterious scout."

"Mysterious!" Ab scoffed. He looked over his shoulder at his nephew. "I never knew that about you, Royal. Mysterious! Did you know that?"

Grinning sheepishly, Roy shook his head.

"As I mentioned," Nichols said, "locating you has been a difficult task, difficult indeed. You served six regiments that I know of, and at war's end you dropped from sight like a stone tossed into deep water."

Roy thought about that. "Mister Nichols, when the fighting was done, I went home." A man of few words, he had no more to say. The two stared at one another until Ab spoke up.

"My brother's farm outside Waterville is well known," Ab stated. "If you had asked around, you'd have found the place."

"I know that now," Nichols said. He turned to Roy. "To cut a long story down to size, I found your family farm and met Mister and Missus Albert Smith. Your mother's a dear woman and your father's a gentleman. They informed me I'd find you on a ranch somewhere on the Colorado prairie, a place called Hat Creek."

Nichols cast a glance at his wife. "We traveled the entire distance by rail. As I said . . . a long journey. This is a wild and empty plain you call home, a land of great vistas to dazzle the eye." He concluded: "Now, at last, a mystery has been solved."

"You keep talking about a mystery," Ab said.

"If you knew how many Union soldiers signed their discharge papers 'R. Smith'," Nichols explained, "you would understand."

Roy saw Anne smile, an expectant look lighting her eyes. She was pretty, he thought, knowing at once the look was not meant for him. A long-awaited moment of triumph in her husband's search, she basked in it.

"I have come to ask about your war service," Nichols said.

"That was a long time ago," Roy said.

Nichols nodded soberly. "Some men won't speak of it at all. Who can blame them? I make no judgment about that. All I can say to you is, I have crossed half the continent to ask your help in completing the official record of a brave regiment."

"Not much I can tell you, Mister Nichols," Roy said. He thought for a moment. "Maybe you know a squad from the Hundred and Twelfth was dug in at Fox Run when they got hit by Reb artillery."

Nichols nodded. "Wiped out to a man, hours after the surrender. Tragic."

"If I had been a better scout," Roy said, "those men might be alive today."

A stove lid clanged when Ab dropped it on the iron stove top. "Royal, you followed orders. You done your duty. You was a fine scout. Anyone who's ever hunted bear with you knows that. You don't miss nothing."

Nichols nodded slowly. "I am inclined to agree with your uncle. I have interviewed numerous veterans of the One Hundred and Twelfth. All of them speak highly of you, including Captain Jacob Keller."

"Keller," Roy repeated. It was a name he had not heard in a long time. He remembered a slender man with close-cropped hair and a broad smile under his full mustache. Fitted with a peg leg from a war wound that had resulted in amputation, the captain could have gone home. But he was determined to see it through to the end, and manned a field desk while keeping corps records.

"He remembers you well," Nichols said, "even though he knew you only briefly."

Roy pushed memories away, or tried to. "Like I said, Mister Nichols, there is not much I can tell you. I was assigned to the Hundred and Twelfth for a few weeks. The war ended. I went home." With a glance at Anne, he added: "I'm sorry you folks came all this way just for that."

The door to the verandah stood partly open. From outside came sounds of laughter amid splashing water. Anne stood, saying she would check on the children. On her way out, she paused behind her husband. She put her hands on his shoulders and leaned close to his ear.

"Tell him, John," she said. "Tell him."

Nichols lowered his gaze. After she left, he stared at the rough pine table top, a surface mapped by the stains of bacon grease and coffee.

"Tell me what?" Roy asked.

"Mister Smith," Nichols said, lifting his gaze, "I shall be candid. My purpose in coming here is a bit more involved than a mere compilation of historical references. Oh, some fine day I hope to pen such a document and record the heroism of the One Hundred and Twelfth. *Regiment of Heroes* is an apt title, don't you agree?" He paused. "But I must confess. I have sought you out for more immediate and tangible purposes."

Roy looked at him questioningly. Ab was silent.

"At the end of the war," Nichols went on, "you filed a report with your captain. According to Keller, you remarked on the presence of two officers, a Union general and a Confederate general. You saw them meet clandestinely in a Virginia forest. Isn't that true?"

Roy corrected him. "I didn't write a report."

"I saw the document myself," Nichols countered. "As you observed, that was a long time ago. Perhaps you have forgotten."

"I haven't forgotten anything from that day."

Nichols cast a stern look at him. A knowledgeable man, he was unaccustomed to being contradicted.

"Mister Smith, that document resides in the official papers of the regiment. I saw it myself in the archives in Albany."

"Mister Nichols," Roy said, "you don't know what you saw."

Testy now, Nichols demanded: "I beg your pardon?"

"Captain Keller called me into the HQ tent that day," Roy explained. "He asked questions and wrote down some of my answers. He printed my name on the bottom of the page. Next day we broke camp. We bivouacked outside Washington. Six days later Captain Keller signed my discharge papers. I mustered out of the Army and went home."

"I see," Nichols conceded. He thought about that. "Well, I suppose I could have been mistaken about the authorship of the report, at least in the most literal sense of the term." He reached to his pocket. "I have something for you to look at."

Nichols drew out two photographic portraits and set them on the stained table. Mounted on thin paperboard and reproduced in sepia tone, such portraits were handed out to family and friends. Each of these showed a general officer in dress uniform—one Union, the other Confederate.

Roy stared. The day was warm, but a chill crawled up his spine.

"You saw these two men that day?"

Roy's throat tightened.

Ab came to the table and leaned over his nephew. "Who are these fellers?"

"The Confederate is Aaron P. Bowman," Nichols answered. "The other is Jay Dean Hayes. Hayes served as adjutant to General Ulysses Grant. Bowman answered directly to an aide-de-camp of Jefferson Davis."

Nichols paused. "According to the junior officers I interviewed, these two men, highly placed as they were, wielded more influence than many field commanders . . . even those who outranked them. In addition, I have learned they were classmates at West Point. Close friends, in fact. In the war both of them moved about freely near enemy lines. It's guesswork, gentlemen, but my theory is simple, born of logic. These two general officers came across one another sometime before war's end, and resumed their friendship. Over a period of time, I believe, they hatched a plan to enrich themselves."

Roy listened, feeling like he had been shoved underwater, plunged face first into a tangled, stifling dream of drowning. He saw himself lying prone, not in water, but on a forest floor of rotting leaves, a shaded place distant in time and terrain—a windstorm shook the trees—a lone horseman appeared. In his mind's eye, Roy saw a gray tunic edged in black and a red sash knotted to the handle of a saber.

He blinked. On a conscious level he knew the sounds of splashing water from Hat Creek had thrust the image of drowning into his mind. He was not submerged in water, or pushed into a hot stench of compost, either. But still he struggled to breathe when he looked at the other portrait.

From a plumed campaign hat to polished boots and cavalry spurs captured in his portrait, the Union general stood before a painted backdrop. It was a dream-like landscape of rounded tree boughs and voluminous clouds. Head thrown back and one hand thrust into his jacket front, he struck a stern, Napoléonic pose.

"You saw them, didn't you?" Nichols asked now.

Roy nodded.

"Did they have a pack animal or some type of luggage?"

"Saddlebags."

"Saddlebags," Nichols repeated with a tone of urgency in his voice. "You're certain?"

Roy nodded. "I saw them heft saddlebags off the Reb's horse and tie them behind the Union general's saddle. They rode off, one toward the Rebs, the other toward the Union line."

A wild look lit Nichols's eyes. "What happened?"

"I went back to Fox Run. . . ." His voice faltered, keenly aware that Nichols stared at him.

"You never saw those officers again?" he demanded.

Roy shook his head.

"So you don't know where they went?"

"No."

"What happened after that?"

"The men of the Hundred and Twelfth had fallen," Roy answered. "From the footbridge, I hiked to headquarters. On the way, Reb infantry came out of the trees . . . the sergeant hollered at me . . . something about a surrender."

"That was how you heard the war had ended?"

Roy nodded. "Those Rebs would have gunned me down if the fighting had still been going on."

Nichols slammed a hand down on the table. He turned toward the open door.

"Anne! Anne! He saw Bowman and Hayes! By God, R. Smith saw them! He saw them with his own eyes!"

# Chapter Two

Water boiled in a battered coffee pot on the stove while memories boiled up in Roy's mind. Preoccupied with the past, he absently watched Ab drop two handfuls of freshly ground coffee into roiling water. The odor of fresh brew soon filled the room.

Roy pulled his thoughts together. He had told John Nichols the truth when he said he knew little of regimental history—at least not in the terms favored by Nichols. Roy pegged him as a man who viewed the past through a maze of testimony and archival records—penned speeches, memoirs, diaries, letters, newspaper articles, official documents—words frozen in time.

To Roy history was personal. The past was intimate, an overlay of memories recalled from childhood to this moment. By his reckoning, the remembrances of his life were his and his alone. He saw nothing to be gained by giving voice to troubling memories. Better, he thought, to keep them to himself.

But now in the moments before Anne Nichols returned to the house, remembrances of battle seeped into his mind. Along with the war, images of the creature loomed in his thoughts. Dream-like, he pictured that small, dark-eyed face staring at him from a cave deep in a Virginia forest—body trembling—eyes fearful.

Roy had not mentioned this sighting to his commanding officers. He had kept it to himself, venturing few details when he had been questioned by Captain Keller. It had been enough to report the meeting between a Confederate and Union general.

The creature was another matter, a being he could not readily name. Roy did not want "madman" or "lunatic" entered into his military record. All he had wanted was to go back to Waterville, back to the peace and quiet and predictable routines of the Smith farm.

At home Roy had never mentioned the creature. He had not even told his family that he had witnessed the meeting of a Union and Confederate general in the forest. It was his history. He put it behind him, the war and all.

Plowing soil in Maine that spring, he skillfully had worked around granite boulders that marked the farm like the tips of icebergs marked north seas. Alone with his thoughts, he had walked in furrows behind the south end of a northbound mule.

He had discovered such mundane tasks freed memories. In unexpected moments he had wept as he worked. At night fragmented dreams had disturbed his sleep. On occasion he had awoken to find his mother sitting on the edge of his bed. Her soft voice had come out of the darkness. She had asked why he had cried out in the night.

Roy had attempted to alleviate her worries. He had told a half-truth. He had claimed he did not remember dreams.

The other half of the truth had been that he had remembered bits and pieces of his dreams. His experiences as an infantry scout had come to life in dream images that were twisted and bizarre. Like stones dislodged by the plow blade, fragments of the past had surfaced in his mind in broken pieces. Dream memories had been at once unreal and all too real.

Roy figured he had left anguish behind when he had gone West. Endless chores had kept him busy, and he was satisfied with the progress of his cattle ranch. From that first day of riding property lines with Ab to this day, when unexpected guests had showed up at his door, he had had no room for memories of war.

So he had believed. Now the memories came back, not seeping, but in a gush. He was powerless to halt the emotional flood, knowing too late his past was neither buried nor exorcised, but merely dammed until an inner dike broke.

Roy sobbed suddenly. His boot knocked over the stool when he stood. Turning away from the surprised stares of John Nichols and Uncle Ab, he strode to the door just as Anne came in with her children.

"Mama, why is that man crying?" Henrietta asked.

"Shhh."

Roy moved past the silenced daughter and staring son. Anne shepherded them into the ranch house. After a few minutes alone outside, Roy hawked and spat as he gathered his wits, marshalling emotions that had surged out of his control. He returned to the table muttering an apology.

"Mister Smith," John Nichols said, "I have interviewed dozens of veterans. Nearly all shed tears upon recalling events of the war."

Anne moved closer and placed a reassuring hand on Roy's arm. While her children observed them in silence, a quiet moment passed. She removed her hand and took her daughter and son outside again.

Roy saw a worried look deepen the wrinkles in Ab's face. Without a word, his uncle brought three mugs of coffee to the table. Roy caught his eye. He managed a smile as he righted the stool and sat down. All is well, Roy wanted to signal to him.

John Nichols spoke. Roy and Ab listened while their coffee

went cold, both of them caught up in this historian's account of high treachery.

Die-hards never admitted the possibility of defeat, much less the probability. Victory would be theirs. Somehow. Never mind grim news of regiments falling back daily, of brave men weak with hunger as they yielded hard-fought ground to the hordes in blue. Die-hards held out hope even when the enemy advance was audible in the distance, even when bivouac fires sent a haze of smoke drifting into their skies. In the privacy of bedrooms, ladies wept as they emptied velvet-lined cases and hidden lock boxes, the last of their jewelry and secret stores of gold and silver coins willingly contributed to the Cause. Willingly, but not without pain and wrenching sorrow.

Together, meager contributions comprised a handsome sum, a weighty treasure presented to President Jefferson Davis himself in Petersburg. Promising a steadfast defense of their land and protection of rights held sacred, Davis entrusted the treasure to General A.P. Bowman.

The enemy, Bowman announced to the gathered ladies, is fattened, over-confident. He reported bluecoats lounging around campfires with plenty of food to eat, plenty of coffee to drink, plenty of blankets to ward off the night chill, plenty of reasons to avoid a fight. Too comfortable, he said with conviction, and too self-satisfied. Only a lean army will attack with fury.

*Fury is ours!* he concluded in a voice filled with emotion as he grasped the handle of his saber, a handle marked by a red sash.

With the urgent call requesting gems and hard currency, a secret was revealed to the faithful: While Grant's army slept, a blockade runner had slipped into the port of Norfolk. The British two-master docked as storm clouds swept over the moon. With British beef packed in the brigantine's hold, the fortune raised by the ladies was payment meant for the sustenance of their brave men. In this, the hour of greatest need, salted beef was worth more than coins and gems.

Ocean swells slapped pilings, and rough waters in harbor threatened the vessel. Off-loading was impossible. Too late to heave to, the captain cut loose and sailed into stormy darkness in the open sea where his crew had a fighting chance to save the vessel. In wind-ripped shouts, his promise to return to the pier was a voice raised against the storm.

Neither ship nor crew was seen again. Like so many other vessels caught in high seas off Cape Hatteras, this one was believed to have been blown into the graveyard of the Atlantic, taking all hands, cargo, and treasure down with her.

Roy had listened carefully, and now he studied John Nichols. "You don't believe that Confederate treasure was lost at sea, do you?"

Nichols shook his head.

Ab asked: "You figure Bowman stole it?"

"Bowman and Hayes," Nichols said. He turned to Roy. "You saw them yourself."

"Hang them!" Ab said suddenly. "Blue or gray, don't matter! A lynch rope! There's your justice for traitors!"

"I have my opinions about the guilt of those two generals," Nichols said, acknowledging Ab's sentiment. "But there is no factual evidence to prove they committed a war crime."

"Where are they now?" Ab demanded.

Nichols pushed the bench back and stood. "Military records pertinent to my research end with the surrender."

"Hold on," Ab said. "Tell me if I've got this straight. You came all the way out here just to talk to my nephew about what he saw in that forest when he was scouting for the Army?"

"I did, indeed," Nichols replied.

Ab studied him. "Out here in the West, we've got a word for gents like you."

"A word," Nichols repeated. "Dare I ask?"

"Loco," Ab said. "You're plumb loco."

Nichols suppressed a smile. "Crazy for plums?"

Ab saw no humor in this repartee. "When a horse grazes into a patch of loco weed, he turns crazy. Foams at the mouth. Mister, there's no telling what a locoed horse will do next."

"With the exception of foaming at the mouth," Nichols said, "I plead guilty as charged."

Roy watched him turn and head for the door with Ab staring after him, for once speechless.

"A man can bear up against success out here in cattle country . . . so long as it don't kill him."

Roy gained a new appreciation for the hard-earned wisdom his uncle had acquired through years of ranching on this great plain. With the warmth of spring settling over the land, myriad tasks on the L-Bar-7 piled up, faster and deeper than ever. Roy discovered a fact of ranch life: The more improvements he made, the more work stretched out before him.

"Maybe this is the year we oughter hire a hand or two," Ab said. "We could post a note at the livery in Hat Creek. Maybe another one in the Plainsman Hotel and one more in Benson's Mercantile. We might snag a cowhand passing through."

Roy nodded. He did not press the issue. They had wooled this subject around before. The odds of finding a qualified cowhand in Hat Creek were long at best. One of them would probably have to travel all the way to Laramie to locate a dependable ranch hand. Was it worth the trip? One or two men pitching in between now and fall roundup, Roy and Ab agreed, would make their lives a sight easier. But it was a luxury that would cost top dollar. Were they willing to pay?

They had talked about it off and on, discussing pros and cons, expenses, and the aggravation involved with housing, feeding, and supervising men. As usual, words did not lead to action, and the subject faded away. Roy and Ab would muddle through another season on their own.

Easier said than done. Roy had forty-two yearling calves to dehorn and more to brand. Horses on the open range had to be rounded up, colts thrown and branded, young studs castrated. He held half a dozen four- and five-year-old geldings in a fenced pasture, strong and range-wise horses to be used through the summer and fall for saddle stock. First, though, the kinks had to be worked out of each one after several months of freedom from saddle and bit and spur.

Even though Roy had sworn off farming, he plowed a small portion of a meadow and cut a ditch downslope from Hat Creek, slicing through sod and turning soil undisturbed since the Ice Age. He made a chute from two-by-twelves and fashioned a head gate to direct water to soil planted in grain.

Added to this chore of irrigation now, garden fences had to be mended where last winter's heavy snow had mashed them down on the brow of a hill. Without wire fencing, a garden in this region fed cottontails and jack rabbits. And somehow Roy would have to find time to lend Uncle Ab a hand with his spring chores. Busy from dawn to dark, the grueling schedule drove Roy to eat everything in sight and sleep like the dead every night.

Since the departure of John Nichols, Roy had given little thought to the war. In truth, a weight had been lifted. He felt relieved of a burden when the rented surrey departed on ruts worn into the prairie by Ab's buckboard. In a strange way that black surrey, itself a funereal vehicle by virtue of color, carried away troubling memories of battle.

As a parting gesture that day, Anne had turned in the seat and lifted her gloved hand. The two children shouted their farewells. John Nichols had not looked back. He drove the team toward the town of Hat Creek, the rig soon disappearing beyond a grassy rise.

Three weeks later Roy came off his range at sunset, surprised to see his uncle's buckboard at the house. Standing in the stirrups, he peered ahead. He made out a hunched figure on the bench seat of the vehicle, and recognized a sweat-stained straw hat, blue flannel shirt, and worn braces. Ab raised up when the sounds of shod hoofs reached him.

"What's wrong?" Roy called out.

"Must be getting slow in my old age."

Roy saw him grimace.

Favoring his right leg, Ab sat up. "Horse kicked me a good one."

"How good?" Roy asked.

"Hurts something fierce, Royal," he said. "It was all I could do to get here. Damned outlaw dun. Should 'a' used him for wolf bait a long time ago. Ride over to my place and shoot that horse for me, will you?"

Roy swung down. He helped Ab off the wagon seat, and discovered he was as light as a bird. He got an arm under him and took him into the house, half carrying and half dragging him to the bunk. Ab stretched out on the sougans and sighed, eyes squinted against pain.

Roy asked: "Busted?"

"Dunno," Ab said. "Sure as hell can't put weight on it, I know that."

Roy pulled his trouser leg up and saw a dark and swollen bruise on his shin. The foot was turned inward. "Can you move any toes?"

"Dunno."

"Try."

The attempt brought another grimace, but no movement.

Roy straightened. "Better get you to a doctor. . . ."

"Let's hold off for a couple days, Royal," Ab broke in. "Laramie's a long way from here, and we've both got a heap of work staring at us. I figure if I can stay off the leg a couple, three days, she'll heal enough so's I can get back in the saddle."

"Two or three days isn't long enough to heal," Roy said, "but it's too long if you need to have a bone set."

Jaw clenched, Ab offered no argument.

Roy did not say so, but he'd seen war wounds turn to stinking gangrene in a matter of days. At least this injury was closed with no external bleeding. Even so, an untreated fracture could leave his uncle lame. The sooner they corralled a doctor, Roy figured, the better. Their best course of action was to board the next Laramie-bound train out of Hat Creek.

With the two of them alone on adjoining ranches, there was little room for error or bad luck. Roy had always known that. As long as both of them were healthy and able to work side-by-side, he figured with a little luck they could handle everything from birthing to herding, from roundups to brandings.

Now Roy shook his head. A dose of bad luck had come their way. The timing could not be much worse.

"What's your thinking on this, Royal?"

"I'm thinking I'd better fill water troughs and spread some grain before we leave. We can be back here in four, maybe five days. The critters will just have to get along without us."

Roy had not traveled to Hat Creek in weeks, and now, by night, the glow of a lamp in the window of the Union Pacific ticket office guided him. Little more than a shack beside the tracks, the structure served as a depot with a pair of weathered benches and several dented spittoons on the ground under the roof overhang.

Roy looked southward. By starlight he saw a water tower, coal bins, corrals, and slanted loading chutes. To the north the sawmill, Plainsman Hotel, and Benson's Mercantile loomed in the night with the other boxy buildings of Hat Creek. Radiating out from the town were residences and small farms.

Roy drew back on the lines. The scent of Prince Albert tobacco smoke reached him. He was startled when a voice came out of darkness.

"That you, Abner?"

Roger Hawkins, the UP agent in Hat Creek, moved around the corner of his shack. He was smoking a pipe.

"Me and my nephew," Ab answered.

"Howdy, Roy. Something wrong, gents?"

"We got us a little problem," Ab replied. "When's the next train to Laramie?"

Hawkins pulled a timepiece from his vest pocket and turned toward the dim light from the window. He spoke around the pipe clenched in his teeth. "Six hours, twenty-four minutes, Lord willing." He turned to Abner. "What's wrong, cowboy?"

"Kicked by a damned outlaw," Ab replied as Roy came to his side. "Me and Royal, we talked it over. Figured I'd better get to a sawbones."

Hawkins moved closer. "I'll give you a hand."

Roy and the agent helped Ab off the seat of the buckboard. He moaned as they carried him to a bench and eased him down onto it.

Returning to the buckboard, Roy took up the lines. He drove to the livery on the edge of town and boarded the horses. By the time he returned on foot, Ab had paid for their tickets and alerted the agent to a job opening for a seasoned cowhand or two.

Six hours was a long wait in prairie darkness, but Roy knew that delay was actually a stroke of luck. Trains did not run to Hat Creek daily, and he and Ab might well have faced a two-day wait here.

Before dawn a mournful whistle announced arrival. Roy stood, seeing the engine's lamp shining like a single eye. The train was on time to the minute. After off-loading freight and taking on water and coal and two passengers, the engine steamed away from Hat Creek into the night, pulling cars and caboose north to Wyoming.

Roy had been dozing when the engineer sounded the whistle. Booted feet propped up on the facing seat, he sat up and looked out the window of the passenger coach.

"Laramie?" Ab asked from across the aisle.

Roy nodded.

A haze of coal and wood smoke hung over Laramie. Stretched across the high plains, the settlement had taken root and grown in the decade after the completion of the transcontinental railroad.

Leaving the coach, Roy swung down from the step to the platform. He helped Ab down. They made their way across the loading platform to the town's main drag. Roy felt jumpy. He looked around. He had not traveled to Laramie for a year, and the steady wagon and horse traffic rolling past them on the street made him nervous.

He had to laugh at himself. A sad case, it was, when a cow town like Laramie seemed like the big city. In truth, though, compared to Hat Creek, it ran full tilt day and night, a bustling and prosperous town supported by rail traffic with all manner of freight and passengers, and many farms and ranches.

He had asked for directions from the conductor, and now he helped Ab hobble along the boardwalk three blocks to the office of Wilbur Ormsby, physician. The doctor took his new patient in right away.

Roy stood aside. Stretched out on the examining table, Ab groaned and gritted his teeth during the pulling and probing.

"Fracture," Ormsby said.

The fibula was broken, he concluded, and the tibia was probably cracked. Large eyes and bushy hair on the doctor's head made Roy think of an owl. Owls were said to be wise, and this one seemed to know his business.

Ab howled suddenly when strong hands forced the bone back into place. By the time splints were secured, he was drenched in sweat, exhausted. The doctor's bill included a used crutch.

"Congratulations, Mister Smith. Make this a long and happy marriage."

Ab sat up. He gazed at the doctor as though he was in the presence of a man gone mad. "Huh?"

Ormsby thrust the crutch at him. "For the next ten weeks you are married to this skinny lady. Don't take a step without her. At the end of ten weeks, divorce her, and send her back to me on the train. Understand?"

Roy grinned when he saw Ab nod. Among other memorable quotes over the years, he remembered hearing his uncle say: "The only word that scares a man more than marriage is divorce." With pain etched in his lined face, Roy wondered if

Uncle Ab thought of that adage now.

Ormsby emphasized the importance of keeping weight off the leg for ten full weeks, even if the distance was only crossing a room at home. If Ab needed convincing, Ormsby said failure to use the crutch would mean another trip to Laramie to re-set the bone.

"Don't you worry none, Doc," Ab said. "I'll dance with this-here bony gal ever' day for ten weeks solid if it means I won't have to see you again."

Ormsby grinned.

Roy left the doctor's office at Ab's side. After initial awkwardness, his uncle mastered the crutch. He negotiated plank walks for half a dozen blocks to a boarding house advertising *ROOMS, Day or Week*.

The proprietress, Miss Ruby, was a stocky woman with white hair bound in a bun behind her head. She informed them one downstairs room was available. The other vacancy was at the top of the staircase. Ab took the first one. Roy mounted the stairs, carrying his grip to a room overlooking the street. He washed in the basin and changed his shirt. Leaving his bag there, he descended the stairs. The door to Ab's room stood open.

Roy leaned in. He saw his uncle stretched out on the brass bed, eyes closed. He told him where he was going and when he expected to return.

Ab lifted a hand and waved without turning his head or opening his eyes. He looks old, Roy thought, seeing the white beard-stubbled jaw and a brow lined by pain.

Roy left the boarding house and walked the length of one boardwalk and then down the other. After eating supper in the Tie Hack Café near the depot, he headed for the livery stables he had spotted. At each one, he informed the liverymen he was seeking a cowhand or two. Only sober, knowledgeable men willing to work should apply.

Harvey Baker, the bearded owner of the Laramie Livery, answered Roy's query in a deadpan tone: "Wish to hell I could find a man like that in this town. I'd hire him myself. Finding two would be a mighty miracle."

Roy was directed to the outskirts where a blacksmith boarded horses "way out there by the poor farm." That was the cryptic description he had received from Baker, and he walked that distance in boots meant for stirrups.

Half a mile away from town, with feet aching, he spotted run-down sheds in a stand of cottonwoods. The barn looked ready to collapse under the impact of the next high wind or the weight of a heavy snowfall. So did a house back in the trees.

As Roy suspected, the blacksmith was no help in finding a cowhand ready to go to work down in Colorado. Roy left his message anyway, and had started to hike back to town when he heard a child's voice. Then another. He stopped at the insistent shouts of two children.

"Mister Smith!"

"Mister Smith!"

Roy was surprised to see the tow-headed boy was William Nichols. Bareheaded, he ran ahead of his sister, Henrietta. She tried to keep up, mouth stretched open as plaits of braided blonde hair bounced against thin shoulders. Faces shiny with perspiration, both children shouted greetings as though discovering a long-lost friend in the wilderness. William reached him first.

"Mister Smith!"

"What are you two doing here?" Roy asked when brother and sister halted.

"We're living on a farm," William answered promptly. He drew a breath. "I have to feed the animals. . . ."

"Not all of them," Henrietta corrected him. "I have to gather eggs in a smelly chicken coop." For Roy's benefit, she added: "It's the county poor farm."

"No, it isn't!" William said.

"Is, too," Henrietta insisted. "County poor farm. We have to stay here for a while. Mama told me."

"I hate this place!" William said. "I hate turnips!"

"We have to stay here, Willie."

Roy interrupted their argument. "Where are your father and mother?"

"We don't know where Father is, but Mama's here."

Henrietta corrected her brother again. "Father rented a carriage. He went to a town called Fairview. We're waiting here. He'll come for us. Mama told me."

Roy looked past them. Movement in the trees caught his eye. Anne Nichols emerged from the grove of cottonwoods, her gaze darting left and right. Clearly searching for her children, she was prepared to call out when she saw Roy. Halting, her hand flew to her mouth as though trapping a secret.

# Chapter Three

In the Tie Hack Café, Roy drank coffee while Anne Nichols and her two children ate supper. He described the injury to his uncle, noticing William and Henrietta were famished. So was their mother.

Anne had politely protested when he had insisted on paying, but gave in after a glance at her children. They shoveled down vegetable soup, fried beefsteak, mashed potatoes, and green beans. During a dessert of lemon pie, the whole building shook when a westbound train arrived at the depot.

Anne nodded in answer to Henrietta and William's request to go outside and watch the train. Wolfing down last bites of the pie and its thick crust, they left the table and hurried out the door of the café.

At the risk of staring, Roy watched Anne delicately wipe her mouth with a napkin. She looked tired, he thought, seeing her brown, caped dress wrinkled and her blonde hair a bit disheveled. Her gaze lingered on the white porcelain dinner plates, all of them clean down to the last smudge of gravy and piece of meat.

"You are very generous to pay for our meal," she said with a glance at him. "Someday I shall find a way to return the favor."

"Anne," Roy said.

Instead of acknowledging him, she stared at the red-checked oilcloth covering the table top.

"Anne, what's wrong?"

She avoided his gaze, clearly debating whether to answer

truthfully or put up a brave front and claim all was going according to her wishes.

He pressed her for an answer. "Something's wrong. What is it? Where's John?"

"Roy, we're in trouble," she said at last.

"What kind of trouble?"

"John. . . ."

"What about him?"

She searched for the right words to explain their predicament. "I allowed John to talk me into staying here in Laramie . . . for safety's sake, as he said. John's no horseman. He rented a carriage when we got back to Laramie on the train from Hat Creek. I packed food and water for him, and he left. That was seventeen days ago. He was supposed to return last week."

She lifted her hands in a gesture of futility. "I ran out of money. I didn't know what to do, so I went to the town marshal. I was naïve to think Marshal Shores would launch a search of some kind. He said his jurisdiction ended at the town limits, and sent us to the county poor farm. He told me to contact relatives and leave town in a week. We've been here more than two."

She drew a labored breath. "I used my last dollar to send a message by wire to my sister. She lives in Georgetown, near Washington, D.C. I haven't heard from her yet. She has little money. I don't know how much longer the children and I can count on the largess of the county . . . but . . . but we have to stay here . . . stay until John comes back."

Roy heard a tone of uncertainty in her voice. "Henrietta told me her father went to a town, some place called Fairview. She said he'll be back soon."

"That's what I believed when I told her that."

"What do you believe now?"

"I . . . I don't know what to think," she replied. "The children keep asking, and I keep giving them the same answer." She added: "I don't want them to see me in tears."

Roy studied her. If it were possible to be frightened, angry, and exasperated all at once, she was.

Anne said in a low voice: "I . . . I simply do not know what to do. I've sought employment in town. I am willing to do anything . . . clean or sew or cook . . . but I have not found employment of any kind."

Her tentative manner and something about the way she said "employment" indicated to Roy that she had never worked before, that these unexpected circumstances had placed her in a position completely foreign to her.

Roy was looking at her, but he was thinking about John Nichols. Now he said it straight out. "You figure something happened to your husband?"

Her lips pursed into a thin line. "I just wish I knew. That's the worst part . . . not knowing."

"Where is the town of Fairview?" Roy asked.

"I don't know," Anne replied. "Somewhere north of here. A great distance. John told me it is too deep in the wilds to risk taking the children."

Roy saw her sitting still, shoulders squared. She was a proud woman—proud, he thought, and frightened to the bone. Kitchen noises and voices from the other diners seemed louder in those moments.

Roy began: "If there was some way I could lend a hand. . . ."

She leaned forward, angling her upper body closer to him. "I want you to leave, Roy."

"Leave," he repeated.

"You had your hands full before your uncle's injury," she said. "Now you have to take care of him and tend his livestock, too. I will not drag you into my troubles. We'll get through this somehow, the children and I."

Roy said: "You've got to trust somebody around here, Anne. Might as well be me."

She drew a deep breath, eyes closing.

"When you came to my place," Roy reminded her, "your husband didn't give me the whole story. Not until you prodded him. Is there more to this deal . . . more than he told me?"

When she did not answer, he said: "Anne, your husband didn't come out West just to talk to me, did he?"

She bowed her head.

"What's his reason?" Roy asked. "Is he going after Bowman and Hayes?"

She did not reply.

"If he aims to accuse anyone of a war crime," Roy said, "he should have a U.S. marshal or two backing him."

Eyes still downcast, she shook her head once.

"Anne," Roy said, "maybe I can help you get a handle on this thing before I go back to Hat Creek. But you're going to have to tell me the whole deal."

Anne Nichols blinked rapidly. She dabbed at tears with the napkin. Then she lifted her gaze. As she spoke, a look of relief came into her eyes.

John Nichols, a young history professor on the faculty of Albany College in New York, chose his doctoral thesis and earned approval from the dean. He would compile historical accounts of the state's regiments raised during the war. The stated motive was to inform the populace of great heroism and awful tragedy in the nation's deepest conflict. His true motive, Anne confided, was not academic, but monetary. He meant to sell a privately printed, leather-bound volume to every possible customer in New York and beyond.

Research uncovered a surprise when the driest of dry military records led Nichols to an archive containing the wartime papers of a Captain Jacob Keller of the 112th New York. Later he found the man. Nichols kept his thoughts to himself while posing questions and scribbling notes. Shocking as it was, he suspected two opposing generals had conspired to commit a theft—and not merely the larceny that went with stores of food and supplies routinely pilfered by soldiers and civilians.

Reaching that conclusion afforded Nichols a sharpened focus for further research. He eagerly tracked the careers of A.P. Bowman and Jay Dean Hayes in stacks of military records—North and South.

Through interviews and a trail of documents uncovered in courthouse basements from Maine to Virginia, Nichols learned the Union General, Hayes, and his Confederate counterpart, Bowman, were more than classmates at West Point. They were close friends, both serving corps commanders as junior officers in the Army until Fort Sumter was fired on. With States voting for secession, one after another, Bowman threw down his uniform and trampled Union blue fabric under the hoofs of his horse. So the story went, a tale widely reported in newspapers across the South.

Bowman went home to Virginia, Hayes to New York. In weeks war was declared by President Lincoln. From that time on, as events of the war unfolded, the separate careers of the two men soared in parallel arcs. In June of 1863 Hayes was appointed adjutant to General Grant. January 1st of 1864 saw Bowman posted to the attaché to President Jefferson Davis.

With the war grinding to a halt in the spring of 1865, the Cause all but lost, Nichols surmised Bowman and Hayes had met secretly. When or where, he did not know. But at some time in that last year of the war they must have conspired to steal a fortune. Whether by design or happenstance, their target was the cache of jewels and coins donated by the ladies of the South in a time of dire need.

Proof of such a theft was sketchy at best. No record of the blockade runner existed, no logbook of a harbormaster lay in the archives awaiting discovery by historians. Bowman claimed a British ship was in port that stormy night, that he had made payment to an unnamed captain. The captain had hurriedly turned his vessel into storm-tossed seas with a shouted promise to return. Bowman never wavered from his account, and no seaman or stevedore ever stepped forward to contradict him.

Nichols sifted through stacks of official documents and opened private diaries in archives and repositories throughout Virginia, only to learn a fact that he should have surmised from the outset: No records were kept of blockade runners. Neither documents nor testimony existed to contradict the word of the trusted general.

Still, Nichols was convinced he was on the trail of a scandal unlike any other in the war. He felt driven to uncover more evidence and conduct more interviews to deepen his research and ultimately to prove his contention—a thesis kept secret from everyone but his wife.

With so many veterans journeying to the frontier after the surrender, no one thought it strange for both generals to retire from service and drop out of sight. No one but John Nichols noted two names disappeared from their respective state and county records at the same time. Where Bowman and Hayes had gone after the war was not a matter of public record—or even interest, despite the fact both were decorated general officers well known in their home states.

Nichols did not know where either man presently resided, or even if both were still alive. Relatives of Hayes were few and distant. Nichols was not surprised when he tracked down fourth and fifth cousins only to learn these shirttail relatives knew nothing about the man who had achieved the rank of brigadier general in the war.

Bowman's family lines offered more promise to a diligent researcher. From landed gentry to sharecroppers, all manner of Bowmans had resided in Virginia for 150 years. A timely interview with an aunt of A.P. Bowman opened a door at last, literally. She opened a closet door, reached to a shelf, and brought out a packet of letters, each one still folded in its envelope. In one of those moments seared into the memory of a researcher, she handed the packet to Nichols while explaining the general's fiancée had left them here long ago. The bundle was secured by a length of red ribbon.

"They were penned by General Bowman in the last months of the war," Anne said to Roy, "each letter addressed to Regina Stans, every word neatly formed on corps letterhead. John pored over them."

Bowman was smitten by this woman named Regina Stans, and claimed to suffer constantly from the "mighty heartache of true love," while counseling Miss Stans to "never again fret over matters of money. . . ." He went on to state his intention to send for her after he had made a new life for them "out West in the far reaches of Wyoming where the world will be ours." He mentioned a settlement called Fairview.

Aaron P. Bowman's plan was grandiose. He meant to purchase large tracts of land for a cattle and horse ranch under his own brand, just as plantations had been founded in the South by ambitious men a century ago. Nichols learned from the co-operative aunt that Bowman had not married Regina Stans, after all. While receiving letters of heartfelt love and anguish from her brave soldier in gray, she had taken up with another man—a scoundrel, of course.

Never again fret over matters of money, quoth the general. Now John Nichols knew.

Still, a wide gulf existed between his certainty a crime had been committed, and proving it by the weight of evidence. He could prove Bowman had penned letters with a quill dipped in the ink of braggadocio, but that was about all.

Returning to the musty archive of Captain Jacob Keller in Albany eventually led him to the Smith farm in Waterville, Maine. Nichols decided to travel out West by rail, reluctantly agreeing when his wife and two children insisted on accompanying him on his "Western holiday". It was no holiday. Nichols was determined to interview a former infantry scout, the mysterious Royal Smith of Hat Creek, Colorado. From there he would travel to a town in Wyoming, a place called Fairview.

An hour after sunrise Roy found his Uncle Abner asleep in the rented room. The gaunt man lay on his back, mouth open. Ab's habit on his home place was to rise at dawn and stoke the fire in the cook stove to get a jump on his chores before breakfast. For him to sleep late in a strange bed, Roy figured, was a sure sign of exhaustion. He saw no reason to rouse him.

Roy had arranged for Anne Nichols and her children to meet them here. The plan was for Ab to join them for breakfast at the Tie Hack. Roy left a message with the proprietress of the rooming house in case Ab awakened and demanded to know where his nephew had gone.

Roy met Anne and Henrietta and William at the door. He

had already convinced her to accept another meal, agreeing to a vague promise of repayment later. Amid morning wagon and coach traffic stirring clouds of dust now, they walked along the boardwalk toward the café.

"That's him," Anne whispered to Roy. "Over there."

He followed her gaze. A stout man stood on the boardwalk across the street. Two mule-drawn freight outfits passed by. Peering through the settling dust in the heavy vehicles' wake, Roy saw the glint of a badge pinned to the man's lapel.

"Marshal Shores," she said.

Roy nodded, aware the lawman watched them enter the café. They were no sooner seated than when the door swung open. Marshal Ben Shores entered. He made his way through the tables and chairs, his jacket unbuttoned to showcase a holstered revolver. He halted opposite Roy. Both children stared at him in alarm.

"Mister Nichols?" Shores asked.

Roy shook his head. "Name's Smith, Marshal."

"Smith," Shores repeated. "Sure it isn't Jones?"

Anne's voice quavered with anger when she said: "This gentleman is not my husband, Marshal, if that is what you are implying."

Shores turned to her, his round-cheeked face set. "Lady, when I want to hear your next tale of woe, I'll send an invite." He faced Roy. "Now, Mister Nichols, I want to know what you aim to do about the return of that carriage and team you rented from the Laramie Livery. Harvey Baker, the liveryman over there, tells me you are overdue by two weeks and one day. Two days now, I reckon."

"You've got the wrong man. . . ." Roy stopped speaking when he was interrupted by the agitated voices of Henrietta and William.

"Mister Smith is not our father!" they exclaimed.

Shores seemed unmoved by the urgent sincerity of two children. He shifted his attention to Anne.

"Missus Nichols, you claimed no one in Laramie could help you. I took you at your word and authorized room and board for you in the county farm. Now I find you in this café, menu in your hand, a gent at your side. Just what is your cock-eyed tale this time?"

"Marshal," Roy said, "you've got no call to talk that way to the lady."

"Lady," Shores repeated.

Roy shoved his chair back and stood. He faced the lawman, fists clenched.

"Just what do you aim to do?" Shores demanded in a low voice.

"You're about to find out," Roy replied.

Still showing his revolver, Shores moved around the table toward Roy. He halted when Anne stood, too.

"Gentlemen," she said. "Gentlemen."

The other diners had turned to find the cause of a disturbance. A pot-bellied cook eased out of the kitchen, heavy ladle in hand as he stood in the doorway.

Roy did not back away from Shores until Anne caught his eye. She jerked her head toward her children. Roy saw fear lighting the eyes of Henrietta. William stared, his face quivering as though he had taken a chill.

Roy sat down and pulled his chair in. After a moment the cook returned to the kitchen.

"Marshal," Anne said evenly as she sat down, "how could I possibly be persuaded to invent a tale that would bring us the shame of living at the county poor farm on a diet of fried potatoes and boiled turnips?"

"I don't know what you would say or do," Shores said. He

turned his attention back to Roy. "You live in these parts, mister?"

Roy eyed him. He did not answer for a long moment. The two men had been close to blows, and tension between them still ran high. At last Roy spoke.

"I run a few head down in the Hat Creek Basin."

"Hat Creek," Shores repeated. "Colorado?"

Roy nodded.

"What's your brand down there?"

"L-Bar-Seven."

"Never heard of it," Shores said.

"My ranch doesn't amount to much more than a patch of grass along the crick. . . ."

Shores broke in: "I've got the Colorado Brand Book in my office. Stay put until I look up the brand you're claiming. You, too, Missus Nichols. Don't move, either one of you, until you get the go-ahead from me."

Roy watched the lawman turn and stride out of the café. He looked at Anne. Eyes flashing, her face was still flushed by anger.

Henrietta leaned close to her mother. "Doesn't he believe us?"

"He will," Anne said. She took her daughter's hand. "We told the truth. That's all we can do."

"Will he put us in jail?" William asked.

"No, of course not," Anne replied, reaching out with her other hand to smooth the tousled hair on his head.

"I wish Father was here," the boy said, frowning.

Anne managed a smile. "I do, too."

"Where is he?" William asked.

"I don't know where exactly," she answered, "but I know he will come back to Laramie for us." She added: "Soon."

William turned to Roy. "Can you find him, Mister Smith?"

"William!" Anne scolded him.

"But, Mother. . . ."

"Mister Smith will return to Colorado as soon as his uncle is well enough to travel," Anne said. She cast a glance at Roy. "He has work to do, and we shall not delay his trip back home."

"Home," William repeated. "I want to go home."

Henrietta said: "We have to wait here, Willie."

Roy saw Anne smile at the big sister and little brother. He heard the café door open and close. He turned when a familiar voice called his name.

"Royal."

Roy saw his uncle making his way toward them, using the crutch to keep weight off the broken leg. Ab had managed to pull one boot on, but the other foot was covered only by a sock.

Roy pulled a chair out for him. Pivoting on his good leg, Ab sat down with a grimace.

"You got some shut-eye," Roy observed.

"Slept all night and half the morning," Ab replied with an apologetic grin. He turned to Anne. "Is it true folks who sleep past sunrise are hellbound?"

She smiled. "I wouldn't know, Mister Smith."

"I've got a bad feeling it is," he said.

"How's your leg?" she asked.

"Still hurts plenty," he replied. He paused and added with a glance at her and the two children. "I'm a mite surprised to see you folks in Laramie."

"We didn't plan it this way," Anne said.

Ab listened intently as Roy recounted the events of yesterday and this morning. When the waitress came, Ab ordered a rancher's breakfast of ham and eggs and buttered cornbread with honey, and coffee. They were all eating when

Shores returned to the café.

Ab saw him coming. He lifted a hand in greeting. "Howdy, Marshal."

Shores nodded curtly. He eyed him. "Abner Smith. Been a spell, hasn't it?"

"Yup," Ab replied. "With Hat Creek growing like it is, I don't get to Laramie as much as I used to. This time I called on Doc Ormsby." He gestured to the crutch leaning against his chair.

"What happened to you?" Shores asked.

"Horse kicked me. Ungrateful outlaw."

As they spoke, Roy saw the lawman mentally put two and two together. He remembered a passing acquaintance existed between his uncle and the town marshal. He watched them regard one another.

"Reckon I should 'a' guessed this gent is your nephew," Shores said with a glance at Roy. "I don't recall ever meeting him."

"This nephew of mine," Ab said, "don't travel much. Mostly you'll find him on his home place."

The marshal offered no apology for a lack of manners, but tersely acknowledged the L-Bar-7 was listed in the pages of the Colorado Brand Book. The brand was registered in the name of Royal Smith of Hat Creek, Colorado. Shores's gaze swept past him to Anne Nichols, and then to Ab.

"Abner," the lawman asked, "what do you know about a gent named John Nichols?"

Ab answered by describing their chance meeting in Hat Creek's mercantile on a Saturday shopping trip. He had overheard Nichols ask for directions to the Royal Smith ranch. Ab went on to tell Shores about their kitchen table discussion later, offering a few details of his nephew's wartime service.

Marshal Shores gazed at Roy, regarding him with an added measure of respect. "You served under the Union flag as an infantry scout?"

Roy nodded.

"Dangerous work," Shores observed.

Roy shrugged. "Luck shadowed me."

"Luck, hell," Ab said. "Ben, this nephew of mine saved the lives of thousands of our boys in blue. Thousands. Don't take my word. Mister John Nichols interviewed hundreds of veterans, and said they all respect Royal."

Shores turned to Anne. "What was your husband's business here, Missus Nichols?"

Roy saw her purse her lips in a facial gesture by now familiar to him. He knew she did not want to answer. But she could hardly duck the question with all of them looking at her, awaiting her reply to a simple query.

Finally she spoke in a whisper. "He was looking for a rancher," she replied, "somewhere near a town called Fairview."

"Who?"

She answered hesitantly. "Aaron P. Bowman."

"Bowman," Shores repeated vaguely.

Ab asked: "You know him?"

The lawman shook his head. "Can't say I do." He paused. "Missus Nichols, your husband should have talked to me before he left town. I'd 'a' told him to think twice before crossing ranch lands up there."

"What . . . what do you mean?" she asked.

"Ranchers are sitting on the powder keg of a range war," he replied. "I'd say Buffalo County is the one with the shortest fuse."

Roy saw the color drain from her face.

Ab broke the silence. "Down in Colorado, we hear talk of a range war brewing. Folks claim it will sweep through Wyoming and Montana like a prairie fire."

"But why?" Anne asked, as though fear for her husband's safety could be conquered if only she understood the particulars of the dispute.

"With settlers fencing off water holes and bringing in livestock," Shores explained, "ranchers' backs are pinned to the wall. That's how they see it, anyhow."

"Who owns the land?" Anne asked.

"That's a loaded question, Missus Nichols," he replied.

"What's the answer?" she asked.

"Let's put it this way," Shores said. "Cattle ranchers and horse breeders have used open range for years. Now it's being gobbled up by settlers, one hundred and sixty acres at a bite, legally or not. Ranchers up there . . . well, Missus Nichols, they won't stand for it. You can be sure of that." With a meaningful glance at Ab, Shores added: "According to talk around these parts, ranchers in the stock growers association held a secret meeting. Rumor is they voted to bring in Tom Hood."

"Hood," Ab repeated with a shake of his head.

Roy expected his uncle to launch into a diatribe, a fiery pronouncement on the subject of vigilante justice. But he did not. Gaunt with snow-white beard stubble on his jaw, Ab sat still, uncharacteristically mute.

Anne broke the heavy silence that had settled over them. "Who's this man, Tom Hood?"

"Dry-gulcher," Shores answered.

She looked at him curiously. "Marshal, I am not familiar with that term."

"Hired killer," he said to her. "Tom Hood tracks his man

and shoots from ambush. Mention of the name alone is enough to send nesters packing . . . some of them, anyway."

Roy saw Henrietta purse her lips in a gesture emulating her mother. William stared at the marshal. Bony shoulders shaking, the boy began to cry.


"Hell, I don't like this any better than you do, Royal. But we've got to give those folks a hand."

In theory Roy agreed with his uncle. He did not acknowledge that fact with even a slight nod of his head or the blink of an eye. Agreeing with him on this particular subject was too painful.

"If we don't, who will?" Ab went on. "Shores won't. He won't set foot outside this town for anything short of a grass fire or cyclone. That Nichols woman deserves to know what happened to her husband. Those two children deserve to know, too."

Roy had never argued with his uncle. Jaw clenched, he did not intend to start now. But what choice did he have? All he knew for certain was that he could not walk away from his ranch.

After breakfast he had watched Anne hike to the poor farm with her children clinging to her like chicks to a hen. Long after they were out of sight, Roy and Ab stood in the recessed doorway to Miss Ruby's rooming house, absently looking out on the busy street.

"Rent a good saddle horse," Ab went on, "and ride to Buffalo County. Talk to the law in Fairview. Talk to anyone who'll listen. If you can't locate Nichols or find out what happened to him, well, come on home. I reckon the missus and her children will just have to live with that." He repeated: "But we've got to try, Royal."

"I can't leave my ranch," Roy said. "Or yours, either. Not

until you heal up."

"I'll handle things," Ab said.

Roy gazed stonily at him. "Handle things. How?"

"I aim to take Missus Nichols and her children to Hat Creek with me on the train," Ab said. "We'll get my buckboard and head for your place. They can stay there until you get back."

"You can't handle chores by yourself," Roy said.

"We'll manage," Ab said.

"Who will manage?" Roy asked.

"When I was the age of that Nichols's boy," Ab said, "I could do ever' chore on the farm. Ever' danged one, from gathering eggs to castrating pigs. So could your pa and our sisters. We milked, sold cream, and made cheese in those days. Smoked hams, too. You've probably heard your pa talk about our growing-up days in Maine. Your aunts are tough as wire. Well, they got toughened up, and so can these-here folks."

"The Nichols family doesn't strike me as farm people," Roy said. "Or ranchers, either."

"Maybe they aren't," Ab conceded. "But that woman, she's got steel in her backbone. You can see that, can't you? What she and her young 'uns don't know about chores, I'll teach 'em. Hell, after you've done a chore once, you know all there is to know."

Roy was thinking about his livestock scattered to hell-and-gone on open range, a fair number of them unbranded. Every ounce of his sweat and blood was invested in the L-Bar-7. For him to entrust the home place to Anne and her children under the supervision of an aged man with a busted leg was beyond the scope of his thinking.

# Chapter Four

Roy listened to the creak of saddle leather and inhaled the cologne of horse sweat. Leaving Laramie, he faced a long ride to Fairview, a ten- or twelve-day trek he had never expected to make. Resolved to it now, he was well mounted on a chestnut gelding showing three white socks. Strong with an easy stride, the horse was the pride of Harvey Baker's livery barn.

Roy followed a wagon road that was little more than twin wheel ruts etched into the prairie. The ruts led northward, tracking the courses of creekbeds, most of them dry. Baker was convinced Nichols had gone this way. Fairview was the only town in Buffalo County, and the twisting route was the one the liveryman had described when the city dude sought directions.

Roy noticed the soil was drier in this part of Wyoming than in his piece of Colorado on Hat Creek. Here a dust plume gave away the location of riders or wagons from half a mile or more, the smudge of dust hanging in the air with no breeze to stir it.

Dry or not, Roy had gained an appreciation of wide-open spaces since coming West. This was the "land of great vistas to dazzle the eye," as John Nichols had described it. Back home, dense forests and thick undergrowth hemmed a man in and shortened his view. Under deep blue skies of the West, grasslands stretched out from all points of the compass. The terrain gave a man a long view, so long that old-timers claimed: "On a clear day a man can see all the way to tomorrow."

Roy wished he had peered into the future. If he had, he would have known arguing with his uncle was a lost cause. He could have saved himself the trouble just by observing the sky where the horizon meets tomorrow.

After a recommendation from Marshal Shores, Baker had welcomed Roy's aid. The liveryman was worried. He described a high-wheeled Dunston carriage, portraying it as the finest vehicle in all of Wyoming—which meant Cheyenne had nothing to top it. The Dunston had arrived last year by rail car. It was an elegant affair. Baker described a lacquered black body with a folding top, an oval rear window of beveled glass, and red-spoked wheels. He feared he had lost his top outfit and one of his best teams to a gent who had presented himself as trustworthy.

Now the liveryman was keen to loan a saddle mount to Roy. He even threw in a ration of grain, all for the prospect of the return of his carriage and team of horses.

Roy passed the time by listening to the calls of red-winged blackbirds and watching yellow and white butterflies float over the surface of rolling prairie. From time to time long-eared jack rabbits loped away, flushed from clumps of sage lining the wagon road. Farther in the distance herds of antelope lifted their heads, some drifting closer to watch him with curiosity.

Cresting a rise, Roy stood in the stirrups to look ahead. The air was still, the plain endless. Dust drifted into the sky. He met ox-drawn freight outfits, five wagons traveling in convoy. Armed with cut-down shotguns and heavy revolvers, the teamsters eyed a lone horseman on this road with suspicion.

Roy gave them room. He spoke to the men as they walked past him, describing the carriage. Had they seen it? After answering in the negative, the teamsters shook their heads when Roy described John Nichols.

"Ain't seen no such a fancy-pants gent," one of the bearded teamsters replied, "or any such a fine vee-hicle on this-here damned poor excuse fer a road."

"Obliged," Roy said.

He watched the teamsters for a few minutes. Their progress was slow even with empty wagons, reminding him of the observation by pioneers: Oxen don't walk, they plod. Popping the silk at the end of a long-handled whip did not change that fact of life. Neither did shouted curses, although loudly snapping a bullwhip over broad backs and venting age-old complaints from man to beast were always worth a try.

With all five teamsters wary of him, Roy wondered if robbery was commonplace on this route. The freighters had hauled goods from the UP loading platform in Laramie all the way to Fairview, supplying roadhouses and larger ranches along the way. Now they were making the return trek with profits fattening their money belts and jingling in their pockets. A man carrying cash in this remote region had reason to be wary, Roy figured. Outlaws could attack and leave teamsters for dead with little fear of the law.

Riding on, Roy thought about the newspapers Ab brought to him every other week on return trips from Hat Creek. Evenings, Roy's habit was to fire an oil lamp and sit in his wicker armchair as he read and re-read back issues of Wyoming papers. The articles rarely if ever mentioned road agents. Like most rags, editorial policies of the *Boomerang* and the *Leader* leaned toward boosterism, with crimes of any type rarely reported.

Roy was armed with a .45 Colt revolver holstered on his cartridge belt. His lever-action Winchester was on the rack back home. He wished he had it now, even though he had seen no signs of danger other than the cautionary attitude of five teamsters.

The long horseback ride brought sore buttocks, leg cramps, and a full measure of reflection to occupy Roy's mind. He thought about the past, his own view of history in particular.

After the surrender, he had craved the serenity of farm life, the familiar chores of his youth. But as time wore on, he had grown desperate to escape the strangulation of dull routines. Letters from Uncle Ab had egged him on, and, when the opportunity came, Roy had left home. Yet now, living on a vast plain far from Maine, he rarely left the L-Bar-7. He thought about that. He had fled the comforts of home to escape confinement. Now that he was here, he stayed close to home.

The dichotomy occupied his mind for a good long while. No matter how much he mulled it amid the steady clip-clop of hoofs, he had no answer, no way to account for contradictions marking his life after the war. All he knew was that he had a place in the world now, a place to call his own.

He thought about Ab persuading him to make this ride to Fairview. His uncle had made a valid point, he had to admit. What if Nichols had met his end somewhere in Buffalo County? The county was vast—equal in size to Rhode Island, someone had said—and human remains could have been buried anywhere, Deceased Known to God, and who would ever discover his identity or know a worried family awaited his return?

Roy remembered Anne's kindness in the ranch house when his emotions got the best of him. He had glimpsed a well of sympathy in her eyes, and knew she understood—perhaps even more than he himself comprehended in those tumultuous moments when he had wept.

In Laramie Ab had congratulated his nephew for making a

difficult decision. Roy had left the rooming house and hiked to the poor farm, bringing Anne back with him. William and Henrietta skipped ahead and waited in the shade of the doorway while Roy took Anne to Ab's room. In there, he stepped aside and listened to his uncle deliver their offer of assistance.

Anne Nichols did not indicate yea or nay. Roy noticed again she carried herself with an air of dignity, a certain feminine grace in her posture and a softness in subtle movements. He pulled his gaze away to avoid staring. No matter how you cut it, he thought, this whole deal was humiliating for her.

Sounds of playing children had reached him, and he turned to the window. Outside, Henrietta and William played a jumping game of their own invention, counting leaps from one plank in the boardwalk to another.

Perhaps sensing Roy's state of mind, Anne declined the offer. But Ab spoke at length, persuasive in his own unique way. Anne reluctantly agreed with the points he raised and underscored. Yes, the children would be better off on the ranch than living like beggars on a poor farm. And, yes, of course, she was grateful Roy was willing to search for her husband—grateful and at once mortally embarrassed by her need for charity.

Roy had kept his mouth shut. Despite high-minded motives, he still disliked the notion of leaving his ranch in the hands of a city woman and two young children under Ab's supervision. Too many ways for things to go wrong. One misstep, and Ab would have to return to Laramie for the doc to reset that leg. What would Anne and her children do then?

It was not a question Roy had posed aloud, but it struck him as a real possibility. He figured Ab was not one to follow doctor's orders for more than a few days, that he would soon be doing chores himself, unassisted, just to keep up with the work. If Roy were a betting man, he would put his money on that one.

After Anne and her children left the rooming house that day, Roy was surprised to learn his uncle was troubled by another concern—this one more pressing.

"Nothing but a scare story, I figure."

"Scare story?" Roy asked, thinking Ab referred to some aspect of Anne's account of the tribulations she had suffered upon her husband's failure to return to Laramie. He was wrong.

"Ranchers bringing in Tom Hood," Ab explained. "You know his game, don't you?"

Roy nodded. "Enforcer."

"A cross between a cougar and a rattler," Ab said, "and they say that's an insult to snakes."

Hood was said to be a dry-gulcher, a solitary gunman paid in advance for his deadly work. He was a legendary figure in the West. In his youth, according to saloon tales, Hood had been befriended by Mescaleros. Lost, tongue swollen, he was dying of thirst when Apaches found him. Water from a hidden seep saved his life.

Tom Hood later rode as a cavalry guide, aiding troopers under orders to confine or slay every Apache clan in the Southwest. Hood revealed secret food caches and springs, remote sources unknown to white men since the invasion by *conquistadores*. Worse, in the heart of desolate and sacred Apache lands, Hood's long rifle claimed warriors who had once saved his life. He was a man with loyalties to no one, folks said.

"A rumor aimed at terrifying settlers," Ab said. "That's how I figure it . . . ranchers scaring off nesters by threatening to bring in Hood." Ab gazed at his nephew. "Keep your eyes peeled anyhow, Royal."

The northbound route to Fairview was dotted with roadhouses. Most were low, log structures under dirt roofs, small ranching operations offering a bunk and meals to travelers as a way to supplement meager incomes. Some were worse than others, according to Ab.

Stop for water, he had advised Roy. "Don't et the slop served in those places, not unless you're set on puking your guts out all night." Ab described the fare as a version of jackass stew, boot-tough meat of unknown origin with turnips boiled in watery gravy. Ladled out of a stew pot, he added, those cauldrons were rarely emptied, never scrubbed clean.

"Hobble the horse and camp on the prairie, Royal. You won't get sick while you're awake, and you won't get robbed while you're asleep. You won't be paying out good money for the privilege of sleeping on some lice-laced bunk, either."

Roy took his uncle's advice. He camped by night. In daylight he stopped at roadhouses to water the horse and fill canteens. Making conversation at these establishments, he described the light carriage and the man driving it. Several folks remembered the red-haired gent wearing a duster and driving that carriage—a vehicle out of place in cow country.

Nights, Roy stared up at starry heavens while coyotes called to one another. In such moments he tried not to conjure up all the ways things could go wrong on the L-Bar-7 in his absence. Worrying was futile. All he could do was to make this ride, return to the home place as soon as possible, and hope for the best in the meantime.

Mid-afternoon of the twelfth day of his ride, a haze of wood and coal smoke marked the town site ahead. Stretching stiff muscles, Roy stood in the stirrups. Chimney smoke lay over the terrain like a dirty blanket. He saw a cluster of buildings under it.

Not much of a town, he thought, at once knowing he should have expected Fairview to be no more than a frontier encampment. Without the lifeblood of a UP rail spur, this settlement had not kept pace with Hat Creek. Drawing closer now, Roy saw a random collection of crude structures, most built of logs and hand-sawn boards, unpainted. In the distance a mountain range shadowed the northern horizon.

Ab had regaled Roy with tales of his youth. Before settling down in northern Colorado, he had roamed far and wide working as a ranch hand in this region. He described mountain forests where pines were felled by settlers. Bucked and skidded downslope, the logs were dragged to the town site, cut to length, notched, and stacked. Gaps were chinked with a mortar of mud and straw. Windows were a rarity. Doors were fashioned from hand-cut boards nailed together and hung in doorframes with leather straps for hinges.

That style of construction was suitable for frontier life two decades ago. More than suitable. From the mud of summer to the ice of winter, log cabins afforded comfort and safety, shelters far superior to living out of a Conestoga wagon. Most emigrants had at one time called their wagons home. They slept on the ground with quilts spread underneath the wagon box. It was commonly regarded by pioneers as a time of suffering while searching for the Promised Land. Some found it. Others turned back, headed for home, "busted" in the parlance of the day.

This was cow country through and through, Ab had emphasized, and such as it was, Fairview owed its existence to wealth generated by ranches. But now with homesteaders moving in, many on the knife-edge of starvation themselves, this settlement had stagnated.

A quarter mile farther Roy made out a livery barn. Across the street from it stood the out-size false front of a general mercantile.

The livery barn and store anchored this end of town. A pair of saloons and half a dozen cribs marked the other end. Shops were packed in between them. Beyond the meager business district Roy saw a scattering of clapboard houses among log cabins, cow sheds, and various outbuildings. Noting hen houses and fenced ground where chickens hunted and pecked, Roy figured roosters and hens outnumbered men and women. In a cabin count, he estimated the local population to be about one hundred souls, no more.

Untouched by a grader's blade, Fairview's main street was deeply rutted. In the spring, wagon traffic had churned mud from melting snows, and by summer the mix of mud and manure had hardened under the sun. He let the horse pick a route over ridges and through ankle-deep ruts. Drawing rein at a pole corral and a water trough adjoining the barn, he dismounted. Roy loosened the cinch. Reaching to his mount's head, he pulled off the bridle and looped it over the saddle. The horse moved to the water trough.

Roy turned and looked up. Barely legible, the black letters of a weathered sign had been painted above the large double doors of the barn:

### BLACKSMITH
### REPAIRS
### HORSES BOARDED
#### Geo. Stubbs, Prop.

Slapping trail dust from his hat, Roy hung it on the saddle horn. While the horse drank, ears twitching, he plunged his hands into a scum of animal saliva, floating straw, green algae, and water-borne insects. He bent over it and vigorously washed his face. After running wet hands through his hair, he scrubbed with a bandanna. Then he filled his canteens and corked them.

Roy looked across the saddle. The area behind the barn was a graveyard for broken-down wagons. He saw split yokes of hickory, ruined harness with corroded buckles, weathered leather straps. Half a dozen damaged wagon boxes and twice that many wheels with broken spokes and cracked hubs lay scattered in the weeds amid torn wagon covers. Taken together, sun-bleached wood and ripped canvas took on the appearance of skeletons and hides, the remains of strange beasts from a bygone era.

Roy saw a man watching him. The gent stood just inside the doorway of the barn. He did not speak or move out of the shade.

"Mister Stubbs?" Roy asked, securing the canteens behind his saddle.

Hatless and balding, he was heavy set with a full beard, silver-gray, neatly combed. He wore a dark blue suit, pinstriped, with a matching vest. A silver watch chain hung in front of his ample waist. In a wordless reply, he gestured to the mercantile across the street.

Roy glanced at the store. Then, moving closer to the doorway of the barn, he held out his hand to shake. "I'm Roy Smith."

The fat man eyed him.

Roy withdrew his hand, wondering if he was hard of hearing or just unfriendly. He smelled whiskey and saw watery, bloodshot eyes. Looking past this town greeter, he peered into shadows inside the barn. A rope knotted into a hangman's noose hung from a crossbeam.

The door to a tack room stood open. Roy saw a lantern

hanging above a workbench and vise in there. The fat man stepped in front of him, blocking his way.

Roy faced him. "Maybe you can help me. I'm looking for a gentleman named John Nichols. You might have seen him. He came through Fairview a couple weeks back. He was driving a two-horse carriage, a Dunston with red-spoked wheels and a black folding top."

The townsman stared at him. "You the law?"

Surprised by that question, Roy shook his head.

"U.S. marshal?"

"I'm not a lawman of any kind," Roy said.

"What's your business here?"

"I told you. I'm looking for Mister John Nichols."

"What for?"

"I have a message for him."

"What sort of message?"

Jaw clenched, Roy fought off the temptation to tell this man to mind his own business. He held his tongue, figuring he needed all the help he could get in this burg. There was nothing to be gained by alienating the town sot, as he suspected this man was.

"Mister Nichols's wife and two young children are stranded in Laramie," Roy went on. "They need him, right away. With no telegraph wire up here, the only way I can get the message to him is to tell him in person."

The townsman swayed and leaned against the doorjamb to steady himself. "I don't know him."

Roy stepped out of the doorway. He went to the corral. Pulling his hat off the saddle horn, he waved it and hazed his horse into the corral. He clapped his hat on his head, and lifted the rails in place. Then he crossed the rutted street toward the mercantile, aware that he was still under scrutiny by the bearded townsman.

The mercantile's false front was intended to make the place look bigger than it was. Stepping inside, Roy entered a store that was little more than an over-size cabin with a lean-to added to the rear for the storage of hub grease, kerosene, oil, and other flammable material. Built of logs with a low, open ceiling, light from a front windowpane played against shadows in the interior.

As his eyes adjusted, Roy saw a cast-iron potbelly stove and coal scuttle in the middle of the room. On either side were rows of wooden barrels and stacks of packing crates. The store's only display case exhibited notions, pipes, cut tobacco and cigarette papers, twists of chaw, peppermint candy, combs, spur rowels. Goods ranging from axe handles to straw hats were racked overhead. At the rear of the store, planks laid across two barrels made a counter.

Roy smelled tobacco smoke. Two men were back there, both hunched over a checkerboard on the makeshift counter. Roy moved closer. The gent with a corncob pipe clenched in his teeth turned to him.

"Something I can do for you, mister?"

Roy introduced himself.

"I'm Paul Scott."

Roy glanced around the shadowed interior of the store. "You own the place, Mister Scott?"

"It owns me," he replied.

Smoke from the blackened bowl of Scott's pipe trailed upward. He was clean-shaven and almost as gaunt as Ab. The second gent, thick through the shoulders, wore a long, leather apron over work clothes. Hatless, his dark hair was combed straight back.

"You must be Mister Stubbs," Roy said to him.

"That makes you a Gypsy fortune-teller," he said, "with second sight."

"A gent in your barn told me I'd find you here."

"Well, you found me. What do you want?"

"My horse boarded," Roy said. "I pushed him, and he needs rest and a ration of grain."

The liveryman nodded without taking his eyes from the checkerboard. "Leave him in the corral for now. I'll tend him directly . . . soon as I whip Paul in this-here championship match."

Roy recounted his purpose for making the long ride from Laramie. He described the carriage and driver.

Stubbs looked at him. "Couple weeks ago, you say?"

Roy nodded.

Stubbs shook his head. "Never saw the gent or the carriage."

Roy noticed Scott was noncommittal, seemingly focused on the pieces on the game board. "Where can I find the town marshal?"

"Fairview doesn't have one of those," Stubbs said.

"Where's the county sheriff's office?"

"Mister Smith," Scott explained, "Buffalo County has never raised enough tax revenue to hire a lawman, much less a deputy or two for patrol duty."

Roy had not considered this possibility. "No lawmen in the county?"

Scott replied: "Folks out here take care of things their ownselves."

Stubbs added: "That noose dangling from the crossbeam in the livery barn will run off most of your tinhorn crooks, bad apples, and full-grown outlaws."

Roy did not miss the message. If one of those categories fit, this was his chance to leave town.

Stubbs swore when Scott jumped three red pieces and kinged. Turning away from the checkerboard in disgust, he got to his feet and conceded the game. Roy caught his eye. His request to sleep in the mow of the livery barn tonight drew a deeper scowl and a vigorous shake of the head from Stubbs.

"One barn fire cured me of that, Mister Smith."

"I don't smoke anywhere near a barn," Roy said.

"I'm not running a hotel," Stubbs insisted. He added: "Leastwise not for two-legged critters."

Roy watched him leave the store. He headed across the street toward his barn and corral. Roy started to leave, but halted when Scott spoke up.

"There's no hotel in Fairview," he said, "but Bess and Jimmy rent out a cabin behind their place." He looked outside before adding in a low voice: "Talk to them about the stranger."

Roy eyed him. "You saw Nichols, didn't you?"

"Mister, I told you. Talk to Bess and Jimmy."

Roy saw him look downward. He could have pressed the storekeeper, but he sensed nothing short of a beating would make him say more.

"Where will I find them?"

"End of the street," Scott said. "Bess and Jimmy run the café and saloon down there. On your right."

Roy left the mercantile. He strode along the plank walk, noticing most shops were empty, window frames broken and paneless. He looked ahead. The saloon on the right side of the rutted street was another log structure with a false front, long and narrow. Directly across the street stood a second saloon, unnamed, too, with a line of cribs.

Roy opened the door and stepped in. Closing it, he was met by the odors of stale beer and damp chaw. As his eyes adjusted, he made out captain's chairs and small tables scattered about the room. To his left, rough planks propped up on packing cases served as a bar. Long-necked bottles lined an open shelf behind it.

Roy looked around. The walls were decorated with mounted deer and elk antlers, curved antelope horns, and Indian artifacts—lances, bows and arrows, and beaded moccasins.

The saloon was serving fifteen or twenty men—a mix of townsmen and cowhands, Roy judged by their garb. Some played cards while others seemed content to sit back and gaze out the windows. The bartender studied Roy from the moment he cleared the batwing doors.

Roy turned and saw a plump woman sitting at the far end of the room. She was seated near a row of stacked beer barrels, spittoon at her feet. She observed him, too, obviously spotting him for a stranger in town.

"Rye," Roy said as he came to the bar. Digging into his pocket, he brought out silver coins and placed them on the bar in front of him.

The bartender brought an amber bottle and shot glass, poured a shot, and collected half a dollar.

Roy downed the rye. He drank another, followed by a glass of dark beer. With casual questions, he learned he was being served by the proprietor, Jimmy Leeds. Roy described Nichols, and saw the man nod once.

"That city gent stayed the night a while back," Jimmy said. "He was looking for a roof over his head and a home-cooked meal. Is that what you're hunting?"

Roy nodded. "Reckon so."

"I'll fetch Bess."

Roy noticed Jimmy moved with a pronounced limp. He was not old, but he looked like an aged man. Hunchbacked and dour-faced, his demeanor suggested he lived with pain.

Jimmy beckoned to the seated woman. She rocked forward and spat a brown stream into the spittoon. Standing, she moved along the plank bar.

"I'm Bess Leeds," she said in greeting. For the accommodation, she quoted a price of $1.50 per night, clean bedding, a towel, water pitcher and basin included.

Expensive, Roy thought, but he was sore from sleeping on the ground, and tired of saddlebag fare. He ate a cold sausage, drained another glass of beer, and settled up. Bess led him outside to a footpath.

Seventy-five yards away a log cabin stood in a grassy meadow—an abandoned homestead by the looks of it, Roy thought. Reaching it, Bess pulled the latchstring and opened the door. She stepped aside.

Roy went in. Dirt-floored, the cabin was furnished with a bunk, a small stove for heat in winter, an oil lamp, and one homemade chair. He came out. Pulling out his wallet, he paid in advance.

Alone after Bess returned to the saloon, he shook out the blanket in search of lice, ticks, and other unwanted critters. Finding none, he sat on the bunk.

He yawned. He had planned to question Bess and Jimmy about that city dude, but now with a real bed under him and a roof overhead, fatigue caught up with him. Bess and Jimmy were not going anywhere, he figured, and pulled off his boots.

He stretched out. Tired as he was, he lay awake. Like an itch just beyond his reach, something bothered him. He was unable to pin down exactly what it was until the whiskey loosened his brain.

Paul Scott and George Stubbs had given him the impression they were engrossed in a game of checkers. But a remark from Stubbs indicated he knew Roy had turned his horse into the corral. That corral was out of sight from the counter in the back of the mercantile.

That meant Stubbs had been watching from the window, and had retreated to the checkerboard when he saw Roy cross the street. Pretending to be involved in their game, the two men put on an act for a stranger in town. Roy felt certain of that. But why had they done it?

The conversation in the mercantile had been stilted, forced. Roy had sensed that at the time, but did not know what to make of it. Now he doubted Stubbs had told him the truth. Scott had hinted of more details, too.

While Roy wondered about that, he recalled his encounter with the unfriendly gent at the doorway to the livery barn. The intoxicated man had asked Roy if he was a United States Marshal. It was not a question so much as it was a statement.

Roy remembered something else, too. The fat man had sidestepped to block him, preventing him from wandering into the runway of the livery barn. Annoyed by the unfriendly gesture at the time, now Roy wondered if something was in there—something a stranger in town was not supposed to see.

He dozed, and finally slept. Awakening in cool darkness, he had dreamed someone was killing a cat by inches. Now he knew the source. Caterwauling fiddle music drifted out of the saloon across the street. Shrill laughter from women and the hoo-raws of men carried to him. Earlier Roy had seen cribs over there, shacks just large enough for a man to pay a private visit to a woman.

He wondered if this was Saturday night. Since leaving Laramie, he had lost track of the days. On the home place he approximated the current date by looking at newspapers brought by Ab. Here he had no point of reference. He did not know the hour, either, but guessed the time to be after midnight.

Saturday or not, late or early, he knew cowhands would ride half the night for a drink and the company of a woman. In the West, overgrazed pastures often ringed settlements, marking locations where cowhands had bunched their herds and left them for a ride into town after dark. As long as they posted a nighthawk or two and returned before daybreak, most stockmen would overlook their absence.

Roy's thoughts returned to his search for John Nichols. Born of a question in his mind, an idea came to him. He stared into darkness. He sat up, knowing he would not sleep until he solved it. Fumbling for matches, he struck one and lit the wick of the oil lamp.

The more he thought about it, the more he knew what he had to do. He pulled on his boots and stood. After strapping on his cartridge belt, he checked the Colt. Holstering the revolver then, he grabbed his hat and blew out the lamp on his way out of the cabin.

# Chapter Five

Beyond the reach of lamplight from saloon windows, Fairview by night was pitch-dark. Roy left tortured fiddle music and the raucous sounds of nightlife behind as he followed the boardwalk. Shops on either side of the street were dark. So was the mercantile at the far end of the business district. Across the street loomed the livery barn, a great, yawning shadow with a horizontal roofline against the stars.

Roy paused before crossing the street. He stood with his back to the wall of a vacant shop for several minutes. Standing as still as a tree, he watched and listened. Certain he was alone in this end of the settlement, he moved away from the wall. He stepped off the boardwalk and by starlight he gingerly made his way across the rutted street.

Roy groped his way past the corral. He found both oversize doors of the barn closed. Following the outer wall, he felt his way to the tack room. He opened that door, and eased inside.

Black as ink, he thought, raising both hands in front of him against unseen obstacles. His foot nudged a nail keg as he moved slowly one step at a time. He had spotted a workbench in here this afternoon, and remembered seeing a lantern. Now the handle of a bench vise rattled when he bumped against it.

Roy's presence did not go unnoticed. The tack room opened into the runway, and he heard a stamping of hoofs and the sounds of horses growing restless in their stalls. One neighed, and others picked up the call.

Roy turned. He reached up. His fingertips touched the base of the lantern hanging from a hook over the work surface. He took the lantern down and pulled a match from his pocket. Striking it, the match head flared.

Roy raised the lantern glass and touched flame to wick. Blowing out the match, he dropped it and crushed the ember under the toe of his boot. Shadows danced around him when he lifted the lantern and stepped into the barn's runway. He was watched by the horses in their stalls, the chestnut brown gelding among the interested observers.

Every stall was occupied, a fact that saved him some time. He knew what he was looking for, and now he had an idea where to start. Striding to the rear of the runway, he moved swiftly, keenly aware anyone outside would see lantern light shining through small gaps in the log walls.

Lantern held aloft, he looked ahead. In the back corner of the barn, a stack of wagon covers caught his eye.

Roy moved closer. From a distance the wagon canvases seemed to have been randomly tossed into a heap. He reached out with his free hand. Grasping the top one, he yanked it off the stack. He uncovered another wagon cover, and pulled that one off. Then he removed a third, fourth, and fifth, at last exposing stiff black fabric. A flash of light caught his eye.

He set the lantern down. That glint of reflected light came from the surface of beveled glass, an oval window sewn into a weatherproof carriage top. Lifting top bows, he uncovered a lacquered carriage body and four wheels with red spokes. With the hub nuts unscrewed, the wheels had been pulled off their axles, stacked, and covered.

Roy had no doubt now. This was the Dunston carriage, a trim vehicle partially disassembled in order to conceal it. In the next moment a scraping sound reached him.

Drawing his revolver, he quickly backtracked and ducked into the stall beside his gelding. Accustomed to him, the horse stood still. Roy pulled off his hat and dropped to a knee.

The lantern he had left in the runway cast long shadows. Roy listened while watching the darkened doorway to the tack room. The sound he had heard could have come from one of the horses, but he sensed it was the scuff of a boot on the packed dirt floor. He heard it again. A figure appeared there.

Roy ducked lower, hoping he was concealed by the side boards of the stall.

"Who's in here?"

He recognized the voice of George Stubbs. Peering through a crack between two boards, he watched the liveryman step into the runway. Stubbs carried a long-barreled shotgun.

The liveryman called out again. The lantern drew him like a beacon from a rocky shore. Stubbs raised the scatter-gun, bringing the business end to bear on anyone in front of him.

"Come out!"

In profile, Roy got a better look at him. Wearing nothing but nightclothes and boots, Stubbs made a ridiculous sight as he walked slowly toward the lantern. He abruptly halted when his gaze took in the stack of canvas sheeting in disarray.

Roy stood. He lunged out of the stall and closed the distance in swift strides. The liveryman heard or sensed his presence too late to react. He stiffened when Roy pressed the barrel of the Colt against the back of his neck.

"Drop the goose gun, Stubbs."

He seemed paralyzed by fear. Roy jammed the barrel against his neck, harder.

"Drop it!"

Recovering his senses, Stubbs obeyed. He set the shotgun

down at his feet. He straightened and looked over his shoulder, scowling.

"Should have known who it was when I heard horses whinnying," Stubbs said. "I told you to stay the hell outta my barn, Smith . . . or whatever name you're claiming."

"You heard my right name," Roy said. "I'm not the one who's lying."

"You calling me a liar?"

Roy said: "You lied about seeing Nichols in Fairview."

Stubbs was silent for a moment. "You ain't so highfalutin honest, hiding in here like some sneak thief. I should have locked the doors. . . ."

"You and Scott made a point of telling me there was no law in this town," Roy broke in. He gestured to the noose overhead. "Lynch first, and ask questions later. That's the way you do things in Fairview, isn't it?"

"If need be," Stubbs allowed. He paused, eyeing Roy. "Folks around here believe you go by another name."

"What name is that?"

"Hood. Tom Hood."

Roy shook his head. "Folks are wrong."

"Others swear you're a U.S. marshal posted out of Cheyenne," Stubbs went on. "A lawman on the prod, they say, tracking down an outlaw. Maybe more than one. Some ranch hands are half a step ahead of the law."

"Sounds like the rumor mill is grinding at full speed," Roy said.

Stubbs countered: "You wouldn't tell nobody if you was the law, would you? Or if your real name is Tom Hood, either."

"I told you who I am and why I'm here," Roy said. "Now I'm giving you a chance to tell me the truth."

"About what?"

Roy pointed with the barrel of his revolver. "Under those wagon covers I found the carriage Nichols drove to Fairview. Now I'm asking you, Stubbs. Where is he?"

"Don't know," he replied. "That's the Lord's truth."

"You lied about the Dunston carriage," Roy said. "Now you're lying about Nichols."

"I tell you, I don't know where the city man went off to. . . ." Stubbs's voice broke off.

Roy eyed him. "Let me take a guess. You know someone who does."

Stubbs answered with a shake of his head.

Roy pressed him. "If you don't tell me, someone else will. Then I'll come looking for you."

After pondering the threat, Stubbs uttered a name. "Archer, Sam Archer."

"Who's he?"

"He ranches north of town. Big spread . . . cattle and horses. Owns half the damned county."

Roy saw a pained look in the man's face, and took another guess. "Including this livery?"

Stubbs's grimace revealed a sore point. "Archer owns this barn along with every tool, spool of wire, sack of feed, and bale of hay up in the mow." He paused. "I was neck-deep in debt when he came to me, offering to pay off my bank loans. Said he'd help me. Sounded good, but now I'm worse off than I ever was. See what I'm driving at?"

Roy shook his head. "Can't say I do."

"Sam Archer paid off my debts for a dime on the dollar down at the Laramie Trust," Stubbs explained. "Now I work for a pittance, and he calls the shots. I can slave for him, or walk away with nothing but the clothes on my back." He added: "Mister, if I could get out of here, I would. Hell, I'd run barefooted."

"Why don't you?" Roy asked.

"To go where and do what?" he asked. "I'm too broke to buy a piece of land, too old to homestead. Plowing, harvesting, tending livestock is hard work, dawn to dark. A man needs a sturdy woman and a hatful of young 'uns to prove up a section. I'm all alone. . . ."

Roy had heard enough. "I want to know about John Nichols."

"A dude wearing a duster and city hat drove that carriage into Fairview," Stubbs answered. "He asked me about some rancher. Wasn't anyone I knew. Then he went to the end of the street and stayed overnight in Bess and Jimmy's cabin."

"What was the name of the rancher he asked for?"

"Boone. Or Bone. Some name like that."

"Bowman?" Roy asked.

"Bowman. Yeah, that's it. A.P. Bowman, I believe. But there's no rancher by that name in these parts."

"Then how did the carriage end up here?"

"Archer's ramrod and his *segundo* brung it in," he replied. "They took it to pieces and covered it up. Said I oughta keep it under wraps until the owner comes back. You saw it. It's still here."

"You didn't answer my question," Roy said.

"Which one?"

"John Nichols. Where is he?"

"I told you I don't know!" Stubbs exclaimed. He drew a breath. "I've heard talk. Folks say he left town, headed north on Archer's road. I sure as hell don't know where he is now. That's the Lord's truth, Smith . . . or whatever the hell your name is."

In the morning Roy came into Bess and Jimmy's saloon and café for breakfast. Bess brought a fork, a mug of coffee, and a plate loaded with cornmeal mush, fried eggs, and sage-flavored venison sausage.

Roy was her sole customer. In contrast to last night, the saloon across the street was silent, windows dark. Cribs were empty in the hard light of day.

While drinking a second cup of coffee, Roy struck up a conversation with Jimmy. He learned of the circumstances that had left the man hunched in pain.

Jimmy had been wounded at Cedar Creek where Union forces were caught by surprise at dawn. Attacked and routed, the bluecoats had fled for their lives, leaving campfires, pots of food, clothing, weapons, and ammunition behind. The odors of meat frying and vegetables stewing had stalled the Confederate charge with greater effect than a fusillade. Hungry soldiers had ignored the commands and threats of their officers, and had stopped to eat and to rummage through tents. Soon junior officers were eating, too. By noon the Union infantry had regrouped under the command of a sawed-off madman named Philip Sheridan. Following their little general, they had charged. Three horses had been shot out from under Sheridan in a matter of minutes. Jubal Early's troops, unprepared for a fierce counterattack, had fallen back, and by evening the aged Confederate general had snatched defeat from the jaws of victory.

Jimmy had taken a Minié ball in that first volley at dawn. Down and bleeding, he had watched Reb infantry charge out of the morning fog like ghosts. One private in a butternut uniform had stood over him—not to bayonet a fallen enemy as it turned out, but to steal his boots and to rifle his pockets.

Jimmy confided that his greatest fear in the war was to be shot in the back and to have his family find out, thereby discovering cowardice. More than shouted commands, fear had driven him to face the enemy in battle, he said, just as pain from his wound had driven him later to succeed in business in Fairview.

Like so many other veterans seeking a fresh start in life, he and Bess had come West with a wagon train. The trek had been agonizing for a veteran suffering from an old wound, but it proved worthwhile. Landing in this settlement deep in cattle country, they had eked out a living, "One nickel beer at a time," as Jimmy said while Bess looked on with a smile.

Roy listened before recounting details in his rôle as an infantry scout. As in most impromptu meetings between veterans, the men spoke laconically of their experiences, establishing a sort of soldierly authenticity before drifting on to other topics. After inquiring about trout fishing in the creeks rushing out of the distant range of mountains, and hunting deer and elk in grass-laden valleys come autumn, Roy brought up another subject—the whereabouts of a red-haired gent passing through Fairview in an elegant carriage.

"He stayed in our cabin where you slept last night," Jimmy said. "Next morning, he came in for a hot breakfast and coffee, just like you did. He asked about ranchers in these parts. Then he left town, whaling on that team of horses."

"Whaling," Roy repeated.

Jimmy nodded. "Hell for leather. He had a notion."

While Jimmy spoke, Roy's gaze took in the Indian artifacts decorating the log walls. He saw a lance with a spear point chipped from cream-colored flint. Beside it hung a headdress missing several eagle feathers. He looked at an arrow and a bow, the latter made with sinew for a bowstring.

"What notion?" Roy asked.

"Well, he asked me and Bess to name off every rancher in the county. A chore, that was. Some of them shirttail outfits don't amount to a hill of beans. We named off as many as we could, then all of a sudden that city gent like to jumped outta his skin.

" 'Archer!' " he yelled. " 'Archer!' Just like that. Didn't he, Bess?"

Roy's gaze was fixed on the bow.

Bow.

It was a moment of revelation, one that must have similarly dawned on John Nichols as he sat in this very place, a man eating breakfast while looking at the same Indian artifacts that had drawn Roy's gaze.

Bow. Man.

Bowman.

A slinger of arrows, Roy thought. In that moment he knew Nichols had figured out Bowman was here, a rancher known by another name in Buffalo County, Wyoming.

Archer. Sam Archer.

Roy rode north, following a wagon road that tracked the winding course of Arapaho Creek—a route recommended by Jimmy. Reflecting blue sky, this stream was half again the width of Hat Creek. Deeper, too. Roy looked into shaded pools where native trout surfaced from the depths in search of insects.

Through the morning he was guided by wheel ruts in the dry plain. Cattle lowed in the distance, peaceful sounds in a quiet land. The ruts led toward the mountain range and the headquarters of the Bar-A-Bar, the brand registered to Sam Archer.

Roy recalled Jimmy's description of the Archer ranch. "A fine, large place, it is," the barkeep had said, nodding pensively while he spoke, "with a fine, large house painted white as snow."

A fine, large understatement that was, as Roy saw for himself at mid-afternoon.

Painted white with a white-columned portico at the top of a wide staircase, the structure was the mirror image of a plantation house. This one could have been plucked out of the Old South and lowered to earth here in the West. Instead of live oaks, the backdrop was a line of foothills banked against the mountain range, distant ramparts dark with spruce and pine forests.

Roy stared. This was a place to capture the eye of any man who had ever gazed at domed clouds in the sky and daydreamed of a castle built on the Great Plains. All the greater wonder, he thought, considering the fact that every foundation stone, every board and nail keg, every can of white paint and all the materials and furnishings had been freighted overland from the nearest railhead—the UP station in Laramie.

Roy pulled his gaze from it and looked around, taking in the most extensive ranch headquarters he had ever seen. Five hundred yards away stood horse barns and outbuildings. Ringed by cattails, the stock ponds were fed by Arapaho Creek amid a network of corrals and snubbing posts. He saw two long bunkhouses, a cook shack and mess hall, and half a dozen other outbuildings—tight, straight, and in good repair—all of them painted white as snow.

As he approached the house, the door opened. A girl stepped out on the portico. Girl or woman? Slight as a child, Roy could not determine her age from this distance. With a quilt-wrapped baby propped on one hip, she waited for Roy to come within earshot. Then she cupped a hand to her mouth.

"Mister Archer, he ain't hiring!" she called out. She gestured toward the outbuildings. "Cookie, he'll get you a plate of chow. Eat your fill. Eat, and ride out."

Roy lifted the reins, halting by a hitching post at the bottom of the steps. From a distance the place appeared to be immaculate with columns of marble. A closer look revealed paint peeling. Like scabs, dark patches showed in fluting incised into wooden pillars, painted copies of Doric columns.

"I'm here to see Archer," Roy said.

She wore a bibbed dress with a lace-edged maid's cap. The cap covered brown hair pinned up under it. She was very young, he saw now, no more than fourteen or fifteen years of age. A sprinkling of freckles across her cheeks added to her child-like demeanor.

"I done told you," she said. "Mister Archer, he's got a full crew. He ain't hiring. . . ."

Roy broke in: "I'm not hunting work. I'm looking for a man. Name's John Nichols. Is he on the place?"

She shook her head.

"He drove a carriage to Fairview," Roy said, "about two weeks ago. I figure he came to this ranch."

"You some kinda law dog?"

"No."

"John Nichols," she repeated vaguely. She shrugged. "Don't know nobody by that name. Maybe he changed it. Plenty of men do."

She gestured again toward the cook shack where wood smoke trailed out of the stovepipe. "Mister Archer, he don't like drifters laying about. Eat your free dinner and move on."

Roy gazed at her. "Who are you?"

"Nosy, ain't you?" She met his gaze full on until the baby protested. Shifting the infant from one cocked hip to the other, she pulled the quilt open far enough to look at the baby's face.

"Ma'am, it's a long ride from Laramie," Roy said, "and I

don't aim to be turned away."

"Laramie?" she repeated.

Roy went on: "I'm asking. Who are you . . . some relative of Mister Archer's?"

She gazed at him. "My name is Martha O'Meara. My relatives ain't none of your business. Your business is to ride out before Mister Archer gets back."

"Nobody ever accused me of being smart."

She smiled until the baby fussed again. With a parting glance at Roy, she turned away.

He watched her enter the house. He neck-reined his horse around and rode to a corral near the cook shack.

At sunset, Bar-A-Bar riders drifted in. Roy stood at the corral, hat off as he leaned against the top rail. He watched ranch hands tend their mounts and head for the mess hall, spurs jingling. Fried elk steaks, beans, carrots, and drop biscuits comprised the menu. He had taken Martha O'Meara up on her offer of dinner, and, after eating, he ignored her advice to leave before Archer returned.

She had been right—"Martha sent me" was all that was needed. The ranch cook filled a plate without a word to Roy. Busy as a circus juggler, Cookie did not engage Roy in small talk. Just as well. He was not in a frame of mind to field questions.

Now a dozen or fifteen ranch hands regarded him as they made their way to supper. Among the last riders to crest the distant ridge was an older man flanked by two cowhands.

Roy watched the trio ride in. They halted at the steps leading to the front door of the house.

He studied the horseman between those two riders. A chill crawled up his back. The man's distinctive manner of sitting his sorrel horse, ramrod-straight with shoulders squared and jaw jutting, hinted of an expectation of obedience, of ruling aristocracy.

A surge of memories flooded Roy's mind—the pungent scent of compost rotting on a forest floor—the roar of a windstorm overhead—a strange creature bursting through the underbrush—the sight of two opposing generals shaking hands.

Vivid in his memory, too, were the gray tunic and a sheathed saber with a red sash tied to the grip—and the Springfield's gunsights trained on the man's broad back. Now Roy watched him dismount, a man who was alive because he had not pulled the trigger that day.

Roy saw him cross the portico in a stiff-legged gait that reminded him of Uncle Ab. The two riders accompanying him spurred their horses and trotted toward the barns with the prancing sorrel in tow. They spotted Roy. Exchanging a glance, the pair angled toward this stranger leaning against the corral rail.

"What's your business here, mister?"

The man who spoke was lean with a thin mustache and pointed cheek bones, a sweat-rimmed stockman's hat shoved up on his forehead. The other rider was smaller, dressed in the garb of a cowhand, too. His gaze was fixed on Roy. Both men halted and swung down.

Roy introduced himself. Neither man offered to shake hands. The taller one spoke again.

"I asked you a question, mister."

"I'm here to see Sam Archer."

He pulled off his hat and wiped his brow. "I'm Buck Brennan, ranch foreman. This here's Mike Dwyer. Hiring and firing, buying and selling . . . all Bar-A-Bar business goes through us. I'll ask you one more time. What the hell's your business here?"

"It's private," Roy said.

"Private, huh?" Dwyer said.

Roy heard the note of challenge in the man's voice, and saw his fists clench.

Brennan said: "I ride with Sam Archer pert' near every day. If he was expecting company, he'd have told me. Now, state your business."

"Or ride," Dwyer added.

Roy eyed them. Dwyer was clearly the more combative of the two, but Brennan's tone of voice left no room for negotiation, either.

"After I see Archer," Roy said, "I'll leave."

Dwyer cast a sidelong glance at Brennan. "This gent don't get plain English."

"Seems so," Brennan agreed.

Dwyer edged closer, fists coming up to his waist.

"I didn't come here for a fight," Roy said.

"Better ride out then, hadn't you?"

Roy did not back away from Dwyer. In the next instant he was down with gritty dust in his mouth and his ears roaring. He looked up at a blue sky, wondering what had happened.

The two men stood over him, grinning. Brennan rubbed the knuckles of his right hand.

His head clearing, Roy realized he had let the man move out of his line of vision. He figured Dwyer would start something, but it was the foreman who had sucker punched him. Roy had not seen it coming.

He got to his feet, staggering. He leaned against a corral post while the earth steadied and the roar in his ears let up.

"Want more?" Brennan asked, flexing his right hand. "Or have you changed your mind about bothering Mister Archer after a long day in the saddle?"

# Chapter Six

Roy glanced back as he left the Bar-A-Bar Ranch headquarters on horseback. Head down, he rode slowly. He wanted to give Buck Brennan and Mike Dwyer the impression he was headed straight back to Fairview and on to Laramie, a whipped man turning tail. He was aware the pair had watched him ride away from the corral. Now in another backward glance, he saw them continue to observe him as he crested the rise overlooking the great white house.

Once out of sight, Roy straightened in the saddle. He changed course. Instead of following Arapaho Creek to retrace his route to Fairview, he left the wagon road. He rode north toward the mountains, skirting Bar-A-Bar headquarters beyond the rise. Riding into the gathering shadows of evening, he studied the terrain, observing the lay of the land like an infantry scout wary of enemy eyes.

The moon was up when Roy cut a small tributary to Arapaho Creek. Nearly hidden by a thicket of willows and high grass, the trickle of water captured the white light of a full moon. He drew rein and swung down. Stripping his horse, he led him to the edge of the brook and hobbled him.

Not risking a fire, Roy made a cold camp. He opened a tin of sardines and ate a few crackers with the oily fish. Chewing was a painful reminder. The side of his jaw ached where Brennan's fist had knocked the daylights out of him.

With nightfall, he stretched out in the grass, head resting on his saddle. Lulled by gurgling water, he looked up at the moon. He found himself thinking about *West of the*

*Moon*, the slim volume of verse he had found in Virginia in the cave under a granite uplift. As in a dream now, the forest creature came to him in a blur, a frightened being fleeing. . . .

Awakening after moonset in the western sky, Roy pulled on his boots. He stood, put on his hat, and tugged at the brim until it was in place. The horse had not moved more than a few paces since nightfall. Roy went to the brook, knelt, and splashed cold water on his face.

Leaving his campsite, he walked back the way he had come on horseback, making his way past clumps of pear cactus and sage. He was footsore by the time he reached an outcropping he had spotted earlier, a stone landmark now silhouetted against the stars.

He ascended the rise and halted behind the granite formation at the crest. Overlooking Bar-A-Bar headquarters, the position gave him a commanding view. From here the ranch buildings were darkened rectangles. A string of horse ponds reflected starlight like pools of quicksilver.

Roy hunkered down and waited for daybreak. An hour before dawn he saw lamplight in the window of the cook shack and presently smelled wood smoke in the air. He did not move until the eastern horizon showed the first light of day. Then he stood and descended the slope, hurriedly approaching the rear entrance to the big ranch house.

Moving past a stinking outhouse and then the ground-level door to a root cellar, he strode toward the back door. Reaching it, he grasped the handle and turned it. He pulled the door open. Roy stepped inside, easing the door shut behind him. He turned and walked slowly into a back hallway off the kitchen. Still half darkened in dawn's early light, the hall led to a great room. Leaded glass windows opened eastward. This cavernous room stood empty but for a leaf-table and a few chairs, a vast space undecorated from one wall to the others. He found a library and sitting room sparingly furnished with a settee and upholstered armchairs, bookshelves, a wine rack, and an outsize humidor for tobacco.

Roy moved past lion-head newel posts and mounted the steps of a wide staircase. At the landing he found a hall where doors to the rooms stood open, left and right. He looked into bedrooms on this floor. All but two were unfurnished, floors bare, dusty and cobwebbed.

See-saw snoring led him to the far end of the hallway. The door to one room down there was closed, and the one across the hall from it stood open. Inside that one he saw a bed with a quilt-covered cradle next to it. Even in her nightcap and ruffled lace collar, he recognized the sleeping figure of Martha O'Meara.

Drawn by the snoring, Roy turned away and moved to the closed door across the hall. He leaned close, listening. As he grasped the handle and eased the door open, the snoring grew louder. Roy peered into the room. Against one wall stood a maple dresser and washstand. He saw a white porcelain pitcher and basin, beveled mirror, folded towel, and a water bucket on the floor. The middle of the high-ceilinged room was occupied by a brass bed.

Roy stood still. He gazed at the snoring man. He had not known what to expect upon his arrival at the Bar-A-Bar ranch house. He figured he would meet a man he could have killed in the war, and now the moment was at hand. He advanced one step, then another. Loose flooring creaked when he crossed the threshold.

He halted. Still snoring rhythmically, the rancher was undisturbed. *Tired old gent,* Roy thought, and for a time he simply observed this man with a beak nose the color of putty and sunken cheeks showing a growth of white whiskers. Images of the gray tunic and red sash returned to his mind. . . .

The man had aged, no longer the robust military officer Roy had seen in the spring of 1865. Even so, he had no doubt this was the Confederate general, the square-shouldered aristocrat in gray he had observed on that last, memorable day of the war.

Amid the ragged snoring came soft, cooing sounds from the covered cradle in the bedroom across the hall. The baby fussed. Roy turned. Floorboards creaked again under his boots. Martha O'Meara sat upright in her bed. Wide-eyed, she stared at him. Her mouth was stretched open in fear, but no sound came.

Roy saw her struggle to inhale. He was frozen in place for the moment, too. Then she gasped, drawing enough air to let out a squeal. Her cry came in a thin, high-pitched voice, awakening Sam Archer.

Roy turned to him. Cussing and coughing, the old man reared up, struggling like a horse in a peat bog. He demanded to know what was happening.

Still gasping across the hall, Martha launched herself out of the bed. She waved a hand at Roy as if to brush him away like a pest. "Get . . . get out! Get out!"

Fully awake now, Archer's blankets fell away from his nightclothes. His gaze was fixed on Roy. "If you intend to rob me, sir," he said, "you will be well advised to abandon your scheme. Leave. Leave while you are able, or my men will. . . ."

"Your men won't do anything, Bowman."

Like a hammer blow to the head, that surname spoken aloud silenced "Sam Archer", and left him staring at an intruder in a state of shocked disbelief. *How can you possibly know my name?* was the unspoken question lingering like the afterglow of a mad dream.

Martha squealed again, repeating her command until Archer raised his voice.

"Leave," he said to her.

"But. . . ."

Archer glowered. "Take the baby and leave."

Martha turned away. She moved swiftly to the cradle. She pulled the quilt off and lifted her baby out. Stepping into the hallway with the infant in her arms, she paused.

"Don't send for anyone," Roy warned her.

Martha avoided his gaze. Clutching her baby, she looked past him and peered into Archer's bedroom.

"Do as this gentleman says, Martha."

A long moment passed before she obeyed. When she padded away, Archer's fierce gaze found Roy.

"Come in and close the door," he said. "Tell me who you are and what you seek."

"I'll give the orders, Bowman."

The rancher flinched again as that name was uttered. "Who . . . who are you?"

Roy stepped closer.

"By god, who are you? Tell me."

Roy heard the man's voice deepen in mixed emotions of surprise and anger. The rich accent was distinct and dignified, the vestige of a gentlemanly upbringing, Roy figured.

"I'll ask the questions, too," Roy said.

"Questions? What questions? Sir, I simply do not comprehend your purpose for invading my home. . . ."

Roy broke in: "Where is John Nichols?"

"Nichols," Archer repeated vaguely. "I know no one by that name."

Roy felt his own anger mounting. "I didn't come here to

listen to lies. I want answers, Bowman. I want the truth. You comprehend that?"

Mocked, rage flared anew in the rancher's eyes.

"Way I figure it," Roy went on, "if Nichols was alive, you wouldn't be lying about seeing him. You'd tell me where he is just to get rid of me."

"Sir, I haven't the slightest inkling of what you are intimating," Archer said. He added: "Any more than I have an inkling of why you are here."

"Call it history," Roy said.

"Sir?"

"History," Roy repeated. "When John Nichols knocked on your door, the past caught up with you."

"Now you're speaking in riddles," Archer said. He raised an arm toward the hallway in a theatrical gesture. "Sir, get out of this house. Leave. Leave, before my foreman comes looking for me."

Roy studied him. "Bowman, Archer . . . doesn't matter what name you're going by. I figure you've been telling the same lies for so long that somewhere along the line you started believing them . . . until Nichols showed up."

Archer glowered again. At once helpless and enraged, the man was clearly unaccustomed to being dominated or addressed in a manner he considered disrespectful.

"George Stubbs told me Brennan and Dwyer hid Nichols's carriage in your livery barn in Fairview," Roy said. "I figure they followed your orders when they told Stubbs to keep his mouth shut. That's the truth. Isn't it, Bowman?"

"I am informing you once again, sir, that I know nothing of this. How many times do I have to . . . ?"

Roy cut him off. "Nichols tracked you from Albany, New York to Fairview, Wyoming. I've been thinking it over, wondering why he came here. At my place, he didn't tell everything he had in mind. He held back."

"Held back? Your place? What the devil are you talking about?"

"It wasn't only history Nichols chased from Albany to Richmond," Roy continued. "I figure it was a pot of gold, a big one. The end of the rainbow landed on your doorstep."

"Nonsense, all nonsense."

"Nichols's research led to Confederate treasure," Roy said. "He came to me to prove you and General Hayes stole it." He asked: "Where is Hayes? Is he on the place?"

Jaw clenched, Archer stared at him.

"Doesn't matter," Roy went on. "Fact is, you built this place and you bought land and livestock with the proceeds of the treasure. Then the day dawned when Nichols showed up. He wanted a piece of it, didn't he?"

Archer maintained his silence as though that alone was an effective denial.

"I figure Nichols laid it on the line when he came here," Roy went on, "and hit you up for a pay-off. That's the only way this thing makes sense."

"Sir, there is not one ounce of fact in your rantings."

Roy knew stonewalling when he heard it, and he aimed to break this one. "Didn't Nichols tell you?"

"Tell me? Tell me what?"

"I'm the one who saw you," Roy said. "I saw you and Hayes in Virginia. You met in a forest. . . ."

A wild look came into Archer's eyes.

"In April of 'Sixty-Five," Roy went on, "I was scouting for the Hundred and Twelfth New York when you rode into a clearing in a forest. You wore Confederate gray with a red sash tied to the grip of your saber. Hayes met you. Union blue and a campaign hat with an ostrich plume, that was his uniform."

They eyed one another. After a long silence Roy answered the unspoken question hanging between them.

"Lying on my belly in that forest," Roy said, "I watched you and Hayes shift those saddlebags from your horse to his."

Archer leaned back, slowly collapsing on the bedding. He lay there, an aged man overwhelmed, his eyes fixed on the ceiling. Roy gazed at him, wondering if he would tell the truth now. The creaking of a floorboard in the hallway behind him came as a warning, too late.

"Get your hands up. Get them up and keep them up."

Roy heard a revolver cocked. He turned toward the voice of Buck Brennan in the hallway.

"I said, get your damned hands up."

Roy slowly raised both hands to shoulder height. He glanced back. Breathing hard, Brennan had come here on the run. He was barefooted and shirtless, wearing trousers with one suspender strap down. Stepping closer now, he yanked Roy's Colt from the holster and tossed the gun onto the bed.

"Reckon I shouldn't have trusted Martha," Roy said.

"I've met jackasses with more brains than you've got," Brennan said. "You're a damned fool for coming back here."

Marched downstairs with Brennan's gun in his back, Roy was followed by Archer, a stiff-legged old-timer still in his nightclothes. Down the back hallway and out the rear door, he was taken to the root cellar. The door to the cellar lay flat on the ground, hinged to anchored timbers heavy enough to withstand cyclones.

Brennan handed his revolver to Archer. Then he bent down, straining to lift the door with both hands. Holding it open, he motioned to Roy.

"Get in there, jackass," he said.

Roy hesitated.

Brennan gestured to the revolver in Archer's hand. "Dead

or alive, you're going in there."

Roy still did not move toward the opening.

"Go on, go on," Archer said, waving the gun impatiently.

Roy's only chance was to rush the old man and wrest the gun from him. But when he saw Brennan's gaze fixed on him, he knew it was not much of a chance. Rather than take a beating or a bullet, he moved to the edge of the root cellar. One step at a time, he descended narrow stairs leading into the cool shade below ground level. The moment he reached the dirt floor at the bottom of the steps, Brennan dropped the door.

Suddenly enveloped in complete darkness, Roy heard a deadbolt lock slammed home over his head. He looked around, or tried to. Whether he turned his head left or right, up or down, he saw nothing, not a timber, or even his own hand held inches in front of his face.

He knew one thing without benefit of vision. The air was dead. He reached out, fingertips touching dirt walls and rough-cut timbers, and wondered how long it would take to suffocate in here.

Probing with his hands, he determined this underground space to be about six-by-eight feet, and empty. A musty smell permeated the air. He stood on the first step and raised his hands. He touched the door overhead. Pressing his palms against it, he pushed, hard. The door did not budge.

He sat on a step, wondering if he could dig his way out. All he had to use for a tool was his belt buckle. He stood. While he took off his belt, he heard drumming hoof beats outside— Bar-A-Bar riders heading out for the day's work on the open range, he figured.

Roy scraped frantically at the dirt around the door frame with the buckle. After several minutes he had scratched a shallow groove a few inches long and raised a blister on his hand. Worse, his breathing was labored. He realized he would run out of air long before he scraped a hole to the surface.

Minutes or hours? He lost track of time and space. His breathing was shallow, and he shivered as though cold. Even though seated, he felt a topsy-turvy sensation of falling through space. Dream-like, he heard a metallic rattle from the deadbolt lock. Then came a voice. Feminine and soft, it emanated from above, seemingly from a great distance.

He listened. As one who did not believe in winged angels working miracles from the heavens, he figured this one was a delusion, the whispers of his own desperate imaginings. Then the door creaked on its hinges.

"Too . . . heavy . . . can't lift. . . ."

Roy heard the feminine voice again. He stood and mounted the first step. Raising his hands overhead, he steadied himself. Then, with his palms pressed flat against the door, he pushed. This time his effort was rewarded by a thin margin of morning sunlight.

He advanced another step and pushed again. The door opened a third of the way. Straining with the effort from an awkward position, he saw fine-boned hands grasping the edge of the door.

Bent down, Martha O'Meara's youthful face came into view. She lifted with all her might while he pushed. With Roy mounting one step after another, the door slowly opened. Martha stepped aside. One last shove, and Roy let the heavy door fall to the ground. It landed with a thud that raised dust. He climbed out of the root cellar, blinking against bright sunlight. Drawing a deep breath, he turned to Martha.

"Please . . . ," she said, wringing her hands in her apron. "Please, don't hit me."

"You saved my bacon," he said. "Why would I hit you?"

"I went and fetched Buck," she replied. She hesitated. "I seen him and Mister Archer take you out here at gunpoint. I knowed I done wrong."

Roy managed a smile as he put on his belt. "Call it even."

She looked at him questioningly.

"You cut me loose, didn't you?" Roy said. "We're even."

She glanced toward the bunkhouses. "The cowhands rode out with Buck and Mike. I heard them two talking. They'll be in the saddle all day, moving cattle and hunting nesters. I seen Mister Archer head for town by hisself." She added: "I brought your gun."

Roy saw her gesture toward the back stoop where she had left the Colt. "Obliged."

"Where's your horse?" she asked.

He pointed at the stone-crested rise overlooking the ranch house. "Over yonder."

He glanced at the open door of the root cellar, and turned to her. With her fine features and the scattering of freckles on marble-smooth skin, she was child-like, he thought again, far too young to be a mother. Rather than tending to the needs of an infant, she belonged in a schoolyard playing jump rope or hopscotch.

"Martha, what will happen to you when Archer gets back?"

She avoided his gaze.

"Will he hit you?"

Instead of answering, Martha spoke urgently. "Take me to Laramie. Me and my baby. Please. Take us with you."

Roy was surprised by her request and the fearful tone in her voice. "That's a long ride," he said. "Too far to ride double."

"I heard you and Mister Archer talking," she said. "You was talking about that high-wheeled carriage with red spokes. You aim to drive it to Laramie, don't you?"

In truth, Roy had not devised a plan beyond delivering the message to Nichols. That done, he would make a beeline for Laramie and board the next train to Hat Creek. Now he reconsidered. If Nichols were dead, what would he say to Anne? What if her husband's remains were never found?

"I reckon somebody will," Roy said.

The vehicle would have to be reassembled, put back together from the top bows to leaf springs, from four wheels to two axles. The team of blacks bearing Harvey Baker's brand would have to be found, too. Roy did not know where the horses were, or even how to locate them. Given his experience, he expected little help from George Stubbs.

Roy turned his attention to Martha. "You saw that carriage . . . here on the ranch?"

She nodded.

"Then you saw John Nichols."

"I seen a stranger," she said. She quickly added: "I'm awful sorry, but Mister Archer, he told me not to say nothing. I was too scared to speak on it yesterday when you done axed me about him."

"Red-haired gent?" Roy went on. "Portly?"

She nodded as though relieved to be telling him this. "He wore a city man's narrow-brimmed hat and a duster over his suit. Shoes polished to a shine."

"That's Nichols," Roy said.

"I heard him and Mister Archer talking," she said. "They was a-setting in the library with their feet up, smoking cigars and drinking brandy."

"What did they talk about?" Roy asked.

"I couldn't hear no words from the kitchen," she replied. "Just voices."

"Arguing?" Roy asked.

She shook her head.

"What happened then?" Roy asked.

"The stranger, he left the house," she replied. "Slept in the bunkhouse. Cookie done fed him. He was gone by sunrise when the hands rode out."

"Did he leave alone," Roy asked, "in the carriage?"

She nodded.

"Which way did he go?"

She pointed to the ranch road. "Last I saw of him, he was headed toward Fairview."

From the house the baby's cries drifted to them. Martha stepped closer. She grasped Roy's arm.

"Please," she said. She let go and swiftly turned away.

Roy watched her hurry into the house. Now he knew. Nichols had left the Bar-A-Bar Ranch headquarters. He had not made it back to Fairview.

Roy had hoped to get away clean, but as he and Martha scaled the rise behind the ranch house, he looked back and saw Cookie. The pot-bellied ranch cook leaned against the doorjamb in the cook shack, watching them.

Nothing to be done about it now, Roy thought as they hiked toward the crest. He figured they had some time. Archer would not discover their escape until his return from Fairview, probably late this afternoon.

They needed time. Roy lugged Martha's grip while she climbed gingerly, baby wrapped in the quilt. Except for the red gingham dress she wore, a tattered straw hat on her head, and high-button shoes on her feet, the brown leather grip held her earthly belongings.

Roy had not wanted her along. No matter how he cut it, she would slow him down in his search for John Nichols. More than ever, he was keen to get back to the home place. He wondered how Uncle Ab was doing, and if Anne Nichols and her children were living in his house and tending his animals. He knew worrying was futile, but still, every delay added to his frustration.

He recognized his obligation to Martha O'Meara. That, and the fact that he had seen her wince when he asked what Archer would do upon his return to the ranch made him realize he could not abandon her. The stab of fear in her eyes was an expression he would not soon forget. Even so, with his help or without it, she was alone in the world, a girl shoved into womanhood before her time. Roy doubted she would be any better off living in Laramie than here in the sprawling ranch lands of Buffalo County.

*Well, that's not my affair,* he thought as they crested the rise.

Martha halted to catch her breath. Roy looked back and shook his head. The gesture drew a questioning look from her. She followed his gaze, and gasped in surprise to see a figure lounging in the cook shack doorway—Cookie. Roy nodded at her, and they moved on.

Their descent down the far side of the rise took them out of sight of the Bar-A-Bar Ranch buildings. At the bottom Roy broke off the branch of a sagebrush. Broom-like, he used it to obliterate their tracks while walking backwards for fifty or sixty yards.

An hour later he found his camp in the high grass. Hobbled, the horse grazed contentedly near the brook. Roy curried him and gave the saddle blanket a vigorous shake. He threw on the blanket and saddle, and then knotted the cinch. He pulled it snug.

Helping Martha and her baby aboard, he adjusted stirrup lengths for her. Not a split-skirt riding outfit, she showed bare legs to her thighs until she shifted her body and pulled the fabric down. For a moment he looked at her and she looked at him.

Roy turned away. With the grip tied behind the saddle and the hobbles removed, Roy grabbed the reins and led the gelding away. On foot he set a course roughly parallel to the ranch road leading to Fairview. He meant to stay out of sight of the road as much as possible. At all costs, they must avoid a chance encounter with Brennan or Dwyer on that road—or with Archer himself.

Their progress was agonizingly slow. The sight of coyotes briefly startled him. Off to his left a pack of gray-brown coyotes milled about, a sight that surprised Roy. In summer the predators were usually solitary hunters. Roy figured this bunch was feeding on carrion—the remains of a steer, probably. An easy dinner had attracted a crowd.

Hiking through terrain cut by gulches, Roy made his way around clumps of sage and pushed through waist-high rabbitbrush. One dry ravine, deep and steep-sided, forced a detour of a mile. More time lost, and then, under the sun climbing to its apex in a cloudless sky, Roy saw dust in the air.

Hearing the bawls of livestock, he halted. From the saddle Martha raised up and pointed ahead. Cattle were under that dust cloud—a large herd pushed by half a dozen cowhands.

Roy pulled back. He led the horse to the dry ravine, and dropped into it.

"We'll give them a couple hours to move on," he said, and took the baby while Martha dismounted. He felt the infant move and then he heard a tiny voice.

The jostling brought cries from the bundled quilt, and Martha took her son back. She pulled the pieced fabric open. She smiled at blinking eyes in a small face, and pressed her lips to the baby's forehead. She asked Roy to bring her grip.

He set it on the ground beside her and watched her kneel

and open it one-handed. She pulled out a diaper and changed the infant. Then, unbuttoning her dress front, she turned her back to the sun and nursed her baby. She smiled at Roy.

He asked: "What's his name?"

"Samuel," she replied. She added: "I done named him for his pa. Frankie, she told me I oughta."

"Samuel," Roy repeated. "After Sam Archer?"

She nodded. "Mister Archer, he don't believe it."

"Believe what?"

"He don't take no claim on this-here baby," she replied. "I done told him it's his. There's some things in this old world a woman knows from her heart, and that's one of them. Frankie, she told him, too. He still don't believe it. Maybe he don't want to believe it. Either way, it's a fact of life."

"Who's Frankie?" Roy asked.

"Her right name's Francesca," she said, "but all of us girls call her Frankie."

"Girls?" he asked.

Martha's face colored. "Frankie owns the cribs in Fairview. I used to work for her." She added: "I figured you knowed."

Roy shook his head.

"You might as well hear the truth," Martha said. "Mister Archer, he likes his girls spankin' young. Frankie said that's why he done picked me. But when I give birth to this-here boy baby, Mister Archer, he didn't take no claim. None a-tall."

She drew a breath. "Frankie, she give him a fair talking-to. Finally he said I could come out to the ranch and work for him. So I done left the cribs. I figured he'd change his mind about the baby, being around him and all. But he ain't budged."

While the baby nursed, she eyed Roy. "Don't worry. I won't trouble you much. I aim to make a new start for me and my son, that's all." She added: "Laramie's a good, big town, I hear. You been there?"

Roy nodded.

"Folks say it's on the railroad," she said, "smack out there on the prairie. That true?"

"Yeah."

"Laramie," she said wistfully.

Roy asked: "How did you end up in Fairview?"

"Wagon train a-crossing the prairie," she replied. "We got into bad water. Ever'body took sick. Ma, she threw up till she died. My two young brothers died hard, too. Pa, he buried them. After that he had sobbing fits and took to whaling on me. Beat me near ever' day. Soon as I heard tell of a town, I run off. Run off in the night with nothing but my grip. A freight outfit picked me up."

Martha paused in reflection. "Frankie, she says I washed up like driftwood on the shore of a sea of grass. How she talks."

In short-lived brilliance, red-orange rays of light fanned skyward from the setting sun. Roy tugged at his hat brim, pulling it down on his forehead to shade his eyes. By the time they drew in sight of the cluster of buildings on the plain, the sky had lost fiery colors. Martha pointed to a windowless cabin at the end of the row of cribs. "Frankie, she lives there."

Roy led the horse along a footpath lined by dandelions. At the door, he helped Martha down and tied the horse at the post. She carried her baby to the cabin door. Roy strode away with a promise to return soon.

He edged along the wall of a building. At the street he paused to check his Colt, a wartime habit. Holstering the revolver, he moved ahead. He looked left and right before stepping out to the plank walk. Turning, he made his way to the livery. The corral was empty, barn doors closed. Across the street, window shades were drawn at Scott's mercantile.

This was the supper hour, and a scent of wood smoke filled the air. Seeing no one about, Roy angled to the barn. He opened one of the outsize doors. He stepped inside. Amid the animal odors in a cavernous barn, he walked the length of the runway. He was watched by the horses. At the far end, evening light from the open door revealed the disassembled carriage was still here, concealed under wagon covers.

Archer's sorrel was not among the horses in the stalls. Roy left the barn, and closed the door. He walked swiftly toward the two facing saloons and row of cribs at the other end of the street. Along the way he noted saddle horses tied at the hitching posts. None bore Archer's brand. Breathing easier in the knowledge Archer was not here, he headed for Frankie's cabin.

Roy strode past his horse to the plank door. He rapped on it. No one answered. Hearing hushed voices, he knocked again, harder. Presently the door opened. Martha appeared there. Instead of inviting him in, she came out, eyes downcast. She was followed by a gaunt, white-haired woman dressed in black. Roy eyed her, seeing facial features sharp as a hatchet. He stepped back to make room for them, noting they left the door open, an uncommon practice in mosquito and deer fly country.

"Frankie," Martha said by way of introduction, "this here's Mister Roy Smith of Hat Creek, Colorado."

He shook Frankie's bony hand, feeling a strong grip. "Good to meet you," he said.

Frankie's sole acknowledgement of the introduction was a terse nod. She wore an ankle-length dress. The collar and sleeves were edged in yellowed lace, decorative material that might once have been white.

Roy was reminded of a snake when he met her steady gaze from small, dark eyes set above pointed cheek bones. He saw a face mapped by violence—missing front teeth, nose crooked, a scar angling across the side of her neck in a jagged white line to her throat.

In the cabin doorway behind her, Roy glimpsed movement. By instinct, his right hand drifted to his holstered revolver. Frankie spoke to him then, her tone flat and commanding.

"I hear you aim to carry Miss O'Meara to Laramie."

Roy nodded. Still watching the doorway behind her, he did not miss the protective tone in the woman's voice.

"We'll see about that," Frankie went on, folding her arms across her narrow chest.

Roy faced her. "Yes, ma'am, I reckon we will."

"Don't taunt me," she said.

Roy met her gaze in silence.

"Frankie," Martha said, "Lord knows, you've been good to me. But I got to make a life for me and my son. Come hell or high water, I'm a-going to Laramie."

"And live by yourself?" Frankie demanded. Without waiting for a reply, she went on: "I can look out for you hereabouts, darlin', but if you go on down to Laramie where filthy railroaders paw at women like you and starched church-goers treat whores like bleeding lepers, why, I can't do a thing for you. Not one thing."

Roy heard a practiced undertone in this heated exchange. He figured they had argued in the cabin. Outdoors now, they rehashed their dispute, an on-going argument with neither of them giving an inch of ground.

Frankie jerked her head toward Roy in a gesture of disdain. "What does this cowboy aim to do for you?"

"I'll take care of myself," Martha insisted.

"You'll have to," Frankie said. "Take your pick of any damned cow chaser, don't matter. You'll get left high and dry. You'll see. You'll wake up alone, no roof over your head, no food for you, no milk for the baby."

"Nobody's made promises," Martha said with a glance at Roy.

"Well, there's one damned thing in his favor," Frankie conceded.

"I don't need promises," Martha said. "Laramie's a big town. I'll find a way to make a living."

"But how?" Exasperated when her question went unanswered, Frankie turned to Roy. "What about you?"

"What about me?" Roy asked.

"I said, don't taunt me." Jaw set, she drew a deep breath. "According to rumor, you're hunting a man."

Roy nodded.

"Who?"

"Name's John Nichols," Roy answered. "He drove a two-horse rig from Laramie to Fairview. . . ."

Frankie interrupted: "You aim to collect a bounty?"

"That's not my line of work, ma'am."

She eyed him. "You look like a cowhand. Just what is your line of work?"

"I own a little spread across the line in Colorado," he replied. "Soon as I deliver the message from Missus Nichols in Laramie, I'll head for home."

"This gent, Nichols," Frankie said, "I never laid eyes on him myself. But I heard tell. Strangers don't come here much, except passing through, and local folks, oh, how they gossip. I heard tell Bess and Jimmy put the gent up for the night. He pulled out next morning, fast. So they claim." She went on: "Damned few secrets in this little burg, mister. Gossip and rumors take up the slack." She added:

"The new ones are about you."

"Me," Roy said.

"Some folks claim you're the law," Frankie said, "a federal marshal who ain't showing his badge. Others say you came here to kill a man, and maybe you already did. Those folks claim your handle is Tom Hood."

"You heard my right name from Martha," Roy said. "That's one rumor you can put to rest."

Frankie shook her head. "Rumors flare up like range fires. Just about the time you think it is stomped out, a gust of wind catches a spark, and flames kick up." With a sidelong glance at Martha, she added: "Rumors about you two will be kicking up, too."

"I won't be here to listen," Martha reminded her.

The two women stared intently at one another, Martha with her jaw set, Frankie with thin, colorless lips pursed. Martha broke the silence.

"Frankie, tell Mister Smith what J.D. said."

Frankie glowered.

"Who's J.D.?" Roy asked.

His question went unanswered until Martha spoke up. "Frankie, if you don't tell him, I will."

"Keep to your own business," Frankie warned her.

Roy asked, louder than he meant to: "Tell me what?"

When Frankie gave no indication of yielding, Martha turned to him. "J.D., he seen Mister Nichols roll into Fairview in that carriage. That ain't no rumor. He said so his ownself."

Roy demanded: "Who is J.D.?"

Arms still folded across her chest, Frankie scowled. Her silence dared Martha to defy her.

Roy saw Martha falter under the pressure of this silent challenge. Eyes downcast, her chin quivered. She fought tears. She wiped her eyes with the back of her hand, a child-like gesture. In some ways she was a child, Roy thought again, a child shoved into adulthood too soon.

Martha made a decision. Turning to the doorway of the cabin, she called out: "J.D.!"

Frankie swore.

"J.D.! Come out here!"

Roy's hand closed over the grips of his Colt as a stout figure filled the doorway in answer to Martha's summons. He saw the fat man step out of the shadows. Emerging from near-darkness inside the cabin to the waning light of evening out-doors, he moved ponderously, like some sluggish, nocturnal creature stirred before nightfall.

Roy recognized the unfriendly gent he had met at the livery. The fat man had tried to keep him out of the barn while claiming to know nothing of a stranger.

"This here's J.D.," Martha announced to Roy.

Roy asked him: "You saw Nichols?"

The fat man gazed impassively at him.

Martha spoke up: "You seen him, didn't you, J.D.? You just told me and Frankie you done seen him."

As Roy stared, a wave of recognition surged through him. With it came tangled memories of war, the sounds and the stench of battlefields still vivid in his mind after all these years. Hatless, this man's silvery beard was combed down to a bulging belly. Instead of Union blue, he wore a dark suit, pin-striped vest and silver chain, and a white shirt with a clean collar.

"Hayes," Roy said in a voice barely louder than a whisper.

The fat man continued gazing at him, bovine eyes slowly blinking.

"You know him?" Frankie asked Roy in amazement.

"Jay Dean Hayes," Roy answered. "General Jay Dear Hayes. Union Army. Retired."

"Get your hand off that gun," the fat man said, "and tel me what the hell you want."

# Chapter Seven

"You know why I'm here," Roy said.

The fat man swayed. His watery eyes blinked while he shifted his feet like a steer on ice to keep his balance.

"Bowman made a ride from his ranch today," Roy said. "He told you, didn't he?"

Hayes did not answer. He had added girth in the intervening years, but the longer Roy faced him on the dandelion-lined footpath to Frankie's cabin, the more his certainty deepened. This man was Jay Dean Hayes. Once a Union general sporting a plumed campaign hat, now he was the village graybeard, reeking of whiskey.

Roy pressed him. "Did Bowman tell you he left me to suffocate in a root cellar?"

"Archer," Hayes said. "Mister Archer to you."

"Bowman, Archer . . . I don't give a damn what handle he's using in Buffalo County, Wyoming," Roy said. "Tell me where I can find John Nichols. That's all I'm asking."

Speech slurring, Hayes said: "I am not acquainted with any man by that name."

"Archer told you to say that?" Roy asked.

Jaw clenched, Hayes did not answer.

"I know you're lying," Roy said.

Aware of beady eyes fixed on him, Roy glanced at Frankie. She stared, still as a serpent. Hayes studied Roy, too, or tried to while his bloodshot, watery eyes blinked.

"Liar," Roy said again.

Seemingly unmoved, Hayes lifted a hand and gestured to

the log saloon facing Bess and Jimmy's place across Fairview's street. "Perhaps I shall discuss this with you over a drink. . . ."

"I don't drink with a drunk," Roy broke in. Fists clenched, he moved a pace closer. "I want the truth, Hayes, and I aim to get it. Now, where's John Nichols?"

Frankie stepped between them. "If you two jokers are gonna bust each other up, take your fight somewhere else. Go on, now."

At that moment Roy sensed Martha's gaze. In a glance he saw her eyes stretched open. He had not thought about it until now, but he understood her reason for fearfulness. She had thrown in with him, and if something happened to him, she would be stranded here with Frankie—and worse, facing Sam Archer's wrath when the rancher caught up with her.

Roy glanced toward the street before turning his attention to Frankie. "Ma'am, get out of my way."

She stepped aside without hesitation.

Placing his hand on Hayes's shoulder, Roy shoved him. The man staggered back, feet scuffing the ground awkwardly. He almost went down. He swung his arms and managed to regain his balance.

Roy gestured toward Bess and Jimmy's place. "Cross the street."

Hayes scowled, refusing to obey.

"We're not done yet," Roy said. "Cross the street. Get some supper and hot coffee in you. I want straight answers before you take your next drink."

Hayes did not comply. His expression was dark with anger. "You can't order me around like some underling."

"The hell," Roy said.

"Money," Hayes said suddenly. "You're after money, aren't you?"

Roy studied him. "Is that how it went with Nichols?"

"What do you mean?"

"Nichols hit you and Archer up for money?" Roy asked. "If that's the way it went, I figure his end of the deal was to keep quiet about the Confederate treasure you stole."

"I don't know what the hell you're talking about."

"You and Archer sing the same song," Roy said. He pressed the man. "Is John Nichols alive or dead?"

Hayes glowered while Martha and Frankie looked on in hushed silence.

"Archer talked to Nichols at the Bar-A-Bar Ranch," Roy went on. "I know that much. And I know you lied to me about him. You saw Nichols here in Fairview. There is only one reason to lie. You know he's dead."

"A baseless accusation!" Hayes said indignantly. "You have no proof. . . ."

Roy broke in: "Maybe not. But I've had a good deal of time to work this thing out."

"What are you driving at?"

"I'll spell it out for you," Roy replied. "Nichols came to the Bar-A-Bar Ranch. He drank brandy with Archer, ate supper there, and spent the night in the bunkhouse. Next morning Nichols left the ranch. I figure Archer sent him to you. Maybe he convinced Nichols cash was not kept on the ranch, that he had to come to you for a pay-off. Either way, he never got here. I figure Archer sicced Brennan and Dwyer on him. Somewhere out there on the prairie that morning they killed him." He asked: "Where did they bury the body?"

Face flushed, Hayes exclaimed: "You have no right to throw around such accusations!"

Roy went on: "What other reason would Brennan and Dwyer bring in that Dunston carriage, take it apart, and hide it in a livery barn owned by Archer . . . and then tell Stubbs to keep quiet about it?"

"I've got nothing to say to you," Hayes said, and turned away.

Roy reached out and grasped his collar. He yanked him around. Hayes staggered again. He caught his balance. He flailed at his adversary like a windmill.

Roy did not duck the powder-puff punches. He absorbed blows on one shoulder and blocked the others with his forearms. Drawing his right fist back, he waited for an opening, and let go. The punch struck Hayes squarely on the chin. Head snapping back, his knees buckled. Roy grasped his lapels and kept him on his feet.

Frankie cursed him. "Proud of yourself? You hit an old man!"

"If he's throwing dirt over a murder," Roy said to her, "I'll hit him again . . . harder."

Frankie swore.

Hayes hung his head. Roy pulled him up, close enough to smell liquor on his wheezing breath. "I can't make you eat supper and drink coffee until you sober up," Roy said to him, "but I can make you wish you had."

Jay Dean Hayes rubbed his chin. "All right, all right. You don't know half what you think you do, Smith. But I shall discuss it over supper."

Roy let go. He watched the fat man turn and walk along the footpath in his unsteady gait. He did not say so, but he figured Hayes meant to cover his tracks. He expected more lies out of the man. In their first conversation, he remembered Hayes had suggested he was a federal lawman as though he expected U.S. marshals to gallop into Fairview at any moment. If Hayes still believed that, Roy thought now, the man would spin a web of lies in an attempt to get his story straight.

Reaching the street, Roy looked back over his shoulder at Martha. She stood beside Frankie on the footpath to the log cabin. Both women stared after him.

Roy lifted his hand. The gesture was meant to be reassuring to Martha, but Frankie cursed him again. He followed Hayes across the rutted street, angling to the door of Bess and Jimmy's place.

Roy sat across the table from J.D. Hayes. He looked around while a strained silence passed between them. From here he could see into Bess's kitchen. Then his gaze took in the Indian artifacts mounted on the walls—a hide-wrapped stone tomahawk, a lance decorated with eagle feathers, and a beaded medicine bag. His eyes stopped on the bow hanging next to a fringed quiver of arrows.

"When I asked Bess and Jimmy," Roy said to Hayes, "they told me Nichols came here looking for a cattleman named 'Bowman'. Jimmy told him no one by that name ranched in these parts."

Brow furrowed and eyes narrowed, Hayes was clearly a man in need of a drink.

Roy went on: "Then Nichols asked for the names of other ranchers in Buffalo County. I figure he noticed that Indian bow on the wall, and when Jimmy said 'Sam Archer', Nichols made the connection from 'Bowman' to 'Archer'. Jimmy said John Nichols jumped like he'd been shot. With directions to the Bar-A-Bar, first thing in the morning Nichols lit out for the place."

Jaw clenched now, Hayes maintained his silence.

Served by Jimmy, a dozen townsmen and cowhands stood at the bar, George Stubbs and Paul Scott among them. The shopkeeper eyed Roy, and shifted his gaze to Hayes. He drained a mug of beer and departed with a parting nod at

George Stubbs. Soon after, Stubbs left the bar, too.

Roy had ordered coffee, and now Bess brought two mugs. She set them down and tentatively pushed one toward Hayes as though expecting him to knock it away. Instead he grasped the handle and lifted the white porcelain mug to his lips. He sipped the brew loudly, scowled, and sipped again.

Bess announced supper. A single entrée comprised the menu—pork sausage and brown rice boiled in dark beer, soda crackers on the side.

"Specialty of the day, gentlemen," she said.

Or the week, Roy figured, depending on how long it took to empty the kettle. He had seen Bess dump in a glass of beer to thin the concoction. Now she brought flatware and bowls, placing the service in front of them.

Roy gazed down at a soft, brown mass steaming in the enameled bowl. It reminded him of a fresh cow pie on a cold day.

Against all instincts he picked up his fork and poked at it. Spearing meat, he took a bite. Supper was lumpy, chewy, smelly. He looked across the table. Showing no concern at all, Hayes ate heartily, perhaps drawn to the task by the flavor of ale.

Roy felt haunted by Ab's account of the fare served in roadhouses. He picked at chunks of greasy meat and probed clusters of rice as though spearing a fresh hatch of maggots, all the while wondering if he would lie awake tonight with pains in his gut.

He drew a breath. Breakfast had been tolerable, and he took solace in the fact that he had survived that meal. All he could do now was hope Bess's cooking was a notch or two above the methods employed by the storied cauldron-bangers of local roadhouses.

Roy looked across the table again. Like a man surfacing

from deep sleep, J.D. Hayes gradually regained his senses while devouring supper. He slugged down coffee strong enough to float a horseshoe, and the time came when he wished to leave. He pushed the chair back and started to get up.

Roy shook his head at him. Hayes glowered. Roy shook his head a second time. The moment of rebellion passed, and Hayes slumped back into the chair, a sullen prisoner, cowed.

Hayes maintained his dark silence while bar customers came and went. Most men filed out later in the evening, townsmen heading for home while ranch hands drifted across the street. The single men made a beeline for Fairview's other saloon, seeking Frankie and the company of women in the nearby cribs.

Bess followed Jimmy as he limped to a pair of captains' chairs at the far end of their establishment. Seated in spittoon range, they both chewed and spat while reading aloud from tattered newspapers left behind by teamsters. They commented on issues of the day, one answering "Uhn-huh" to the other.

Hayes let out a rumbling belch. Roy turned to him. The fat man pushed his empty bowl away. He leaned back, lacing his fingers midway across his belly while his chin drew into folds of flesh.

"All right," Hayes said, as though that one phrase was all that was required to explain himself.

"All right, what?" Roy asked.

"Let's settle this thing," he said. "You had the temerity to publicly accuse me of lying. Called me a liar not once, but twice, you did." A self-satisfied expression of superiority settled over his bearded face. "We both know you are the one who is dishonest, don't we? And a bully at that."

Roy had figured this was coming. He listened to the fat man casually twist the truth as though braiding whang leather.

"From what I gather," Hayes said, "during the war you claim to have witnessed some sort of secret meeting between general officers in a Virginia forest. . . ."

Roy interrupted: "That's one."

"One what?"

"One straight answer," Roy replied. "You admit you talked to Archer today."

"I neither admit to nor deny your specious contentions," Hayes said. "I am merely establishing the truth."

Roy asked: "What's your version?"

"You have echoed lies spread by Nichols," Hayes replied, "a so-called scholar claiming to have uncovered the existence of some vast Confederate treasure. He leveled scurrilous accusations against Sam Archer and against me, and you have repeated them. As to whether I lied to you when we first met at the livery barn, I did not know who you were or why you had come to Fairview. That is the reason I did not answer when you asked if I had seen a stranger in town." He concluded: "I admit to that fabrication by omission, minor as it is."

Roy held up two fingers. "That makes two more or less straight answers. Now, tell me what you know about John Nichols."

"You listen to me!" Hayes said in mounting anger. "I do not believe for a moment that you came here to pass along a message to Mister Nichols. You mean to cash in on a treasure. That's the unvarnished truth, is it not?"

"Not," Roy said.

"Your denial only deepens the lie," Hayes said. He leaned toward him. "Listen to me, and listen closely. There is no treasure. Not one coin, not one gem, nothing. Do you hear me?"

Roy turned. He caught Bess's eye, and pointed to his coffee mug.

Cheek bulging with chaw, Bess spat a long, brown stream into the brass spittoon. She left her chair and strode into the kitchen, presently returning with the coffee pot.

Hayes drew back as she poured the brew. "I can hold no more."

"Drink it," Roy said. "Keep drinking it until the truth comes out of your mouth."

"You talk endlessly about the truth!" Hayes exclaimed, anger flashing in his bloodshot eyes. "What do you know of the truth?"

Eyeing both men, Bess eased away from the table. She turned and swiftly headed for the kitchen, coffee pot in hand.

"Since the day Bowman changed his name," Roy said, "I figure you've both told a stack of lies. When do you aim to tell the truth?"

Scowling, Hayes rocked forward and slammed both hands down on the table top. With surprising speed and agility, he kicked his chair back. He stood. "You, sir, are the liar!"

Roy gazed up at a man feigning indignation, and recalled an adage cited by Uncle Ab: The pot calls the kettle black, he said, because a liar figures the world is filled with bald-faced liars just like him.

"Sit down," Roy said, aware now that Bess watched warily from the kitchen. Across the room Jimmy had turned in his chair. He stared at them.

Roy said again: "Sit down."

"I will not take orders from the likes of you," Hayes said, his face flushed.

"The hell." Roy pushed his chair back and stood. "Sit

down before I knock you down."

"No fighting in here!" Jimmy called out. "No fighting!"

His gaze steady now, Hayes edged away from the table. "You won't bully me again. . . ."

Roy moved to his left and cut him off. "A sash was tied to the handle of his saber."

Hayes halted. "Sash? Saber? Who the hell are you talking about?"

"General A.P. Bowman," Roy said. "I saw him that day in April of 'Sixty-Five." He added: "I saw you, too."

Hayes drew back a step, his face beading with sweat.

"When you met him in that forest in Virginia," Roy went on, "a sash was tied to the grip of Bowman's sword. I saw a plume in your hat."

Hayes eyed him with suspicion. "You have proved nothing. Nichols could have used portraits to inform you of such details in our uniforms."

Roy thought about that. Memories of that last day of the war came to him like a waking dream, a vision at once vivid and unreal.

"Nichols didn't know about the creature," he said.

"Creature," Hayes repeated.

"You and Bowman flushed a creature from the brush that day," Roy said. "I saw a dark figure running through the trees. Reckon you saw him, too."

Hayes stared as though struck dumb. This was a moment of truth, a lightning flash of incontrovertible proof. Cast in its brilliance, the lies that had gone before turned to ash. Hayes could neither draw a breath to refute the truth, nor find words to deny it.

Roy watched him move back to the chair. The man sat down heavily, jaw slack. He picked up a napkin and wiped his face.

"I saw a human form," Roy went on. "Dark eyes, black hair, skinny limbs . . . quick as a flash through the trees and brush."

Hayes nodded slowly. "I saw it. I have often wondered about it. Runt of the litter, likely."

"Runt," Roy repeated. "What do you mean?"

"Born to slaveholders," Hayes answered, "a mulatto runt no one wanted, a castaway forced to live in that dark forest."

In the night Roy suffered from burning hot runs in his bowels. Rolling out of the bunk in the cabin, he mounted a full-scale retreat by starlight to the outhouse. Trousers down to his ankles, he was seated in odorous darkness when low voices drifted to him.

At first he believed cowhands were headed to the raucous saloon across the street. He heard two men, one speaking in low tones to the other. In the next instant he heard the door to Bess and Jimmy's log cabin kicked open, a loud clatter of boards knocked loose from leather strap hinges. That noise was followed by two shotgun blasts, louder yet, one after another. In the aftermath, a long silence was broken by a chorus of shouts. Men called to one another, all demanding to know what had happened.

Pulling up his trousers, Roy lunged out of the outhouse. He joined the group of men crowding the doorway of the cabin. Jimmy elbowed his way through them. He alone carried a lantern.

Holding it aloft, Jimmy edged through the doorway. He moved into the cabin with the deliberation of a man expecting to find gore, a bloodied corpse sprawled across the bunk.

"Nobody's here," Jimmy said in amazement. He leaned down. With his free hand, he lifted the corner of a shotgunned blanket to expose a thin straw pallet. Turning, he looked at the men gathered outside.

"Where the hell's that Smith gent?" Jimmy asked.

Roy stepped into wavering light cast by the lantern. "Here."

Jimmy faced him. "Somebody tried to kill you!"

"Missed," Roy said.

"But . . . but . . . where were you?" Jimmy asked.

Roy jerked his thumb over his shoulder. "Supper went right through me."

By starlight, the barkeep looked at the angular silhouette of the outdoor toilet forty yards distant. He understood immediately.

"With Bess's cooking," Jimmy allowed, "supper goes straight through, hissing and steaming out of the bowels like a locomotive out of a tunnel at full throttle."

"Stinging hot, too," Roy added.

Jimmy nodded slowly. "Soda crackers cool it down a mite."

Roy gave that some thought. "Reckon I should thank your missus for saving my life."

"Her cooking scours the innards proper," Jimmy said with a note of pride in his voice. "Keeps a man healthy in the lower reaches."

Scoured or not, Roy slept soundly for the rest of the night. He awakened under the pellet-peppered blanket long after sunrise. He took a late breakfast in Bess and Jimmy's place, shrugging in answer to their blunt question.

"Mister Smith, who wants you dead?"

Roy had mulled it over. He remembered the gun carried by George Stubbs, and wondered if those two voices he had heard from the outhouse last night belonged to Stubbs and his friend, Paul Scott. In the aftermath of the shooting, he had not seen either man in the crowd.

It seemed unlikely they had tried to murder him in his sleep, though. What would they gain? Or if they had been hired for the job, who paid them—J.D. Hayes? Sam Archer? Those connections seemed improbable, too.

As to the weapon, Roy considered an obvious fact. Most men owned a shotgun. Some owned two or three, along with a deer rifle, fishing gear, and traps. A common practice was to use a light shotgun for bagging prairie chickens and rabbits, and a heavier gun for knocking the Christmas goose out of a wintry sky.

Jimmy looked up from the bar when the door opened. " 'Morning, Mister Hayes," he said.

Roy turned from his breakfast plate to see the fat man step through the doorway. He came to Roy's table.

"Mind if I join you?" he asked.

Roy noted the man's eyes were bloodshot, but not tearing as they had been yesterday. He was steady on his feet, too. When Roy nodded, Hayes pulled out a chair and sat across the table from him.

"It's early in the morning for me," Hayes said, "but I thought I might catch you here."

Roy eyed him.

"I suppose everyone in town knows what happened last night," Hayes went on. "Question is, who did it?"

"Wish I knew," Roy said.

Hayes cleared his throat. "We have our differences, Smith, but I want you to know I am not a man to resort to murder to resolve disputes." He added: "You may not believe this, but neither is Sam Archer."

"You're right," Roy said. "I don't believe it. A cornered rat always fights."

Hayes lifted a hand. "Allow me to continue. As to the

whereabouts of Mister Nichols, I ask that you consider a proposal. Perhaps we can reach an understanding on the subject once and for all."

"I'll understand the truth," Roy said.

Hayes said: "Just hear me out."

"What's your proposal?" Roy asked.

"We shall go to the Bar-A-Bar Ranch," he replied, "and you will hear the truth from Sam and from me. Judge the facts for yourself."

"Go to hell," Roy said.

Hayes was taken aback.

"I won't make that ride again," Roy said. "Not after Archer and his ramrod marched me into a root cellar at gunpoint. They left me for dead."

"Perhaps not," he said.

"You weren't there, Hayes."

"I know Sam returned to his ranch to free you," he said. "He meant to throw a scare into you, and run you out of the county."

"I don't run," Roy said.

"By now, no one in Fairview doubts that," Hayes said. He paused in thought. "The war left some men broken in mind and body, others strengthened. Seems to me, your service as an infantry scout seared you."

Uncertain what he meant by that, Roy heard a measure of respect in the man's voice.

Hayes went on: "As to the matter of the so-called 'Confederate treasure', you will hear the truth from Sam and me."

Roy did not reply immediately. Hayes had him pegged wrong. He had no interest in claiming a share of a treasure, Confederate or otherwise. His sole treasure was the rolling grasslands of the L-Bar-7 in the Hat Creek Basin. At once, though, he figured Hayes and Archer were his best sources of information about the fate of John Nichols.

Still, he had no intention of riding to the Bar-A-Bar—not until J.D. Hayes thrust out his right hand. After a contemplative moment, eye to eye and man to man, Roy shook hands with him.

# Chapter Eight

Roy shared the buggy seat with the fat man. With Jay Dean Hayes at his side, he crossed Bar-A-Bar range on the north-bound road from Fairview.

In the distance, dark birds circled in a cloudless sky. The day had turned hot well before noon, and now the birds swooped in, searching for carrion like roaming outlaws while stately hawks soared high overhead.

Just as Roy would never have believed he would ride from Laramie to Fairview on behalf of Anne Nichols, now he was making another trip that he could not have foreseen only hours earlier. Reins in hand, he looked beyond the twitching ears of the team of horses from Stubbs's livery while Hayes talked in a steady monologue.

All hope for reconciliation was lost. The North and South were forever cleaved when General George McClellan was defeated by Abraham Lincoln, the politician McClellan called "nothing more than a well-meaning baboon." Men would die not by the thousands, he predicted, but by the tens of thousands.

Confederate General A.P. Bowman and Union General Jay Dean Hayes shared this view. After Lincoln's election to a second term, dire predictions of death and destruction came to pass. Murderous battles were waged on land and at sea. The country had lapsed into a war seemingly without end.

The Union would be preserved, slavery abolished. Lincoln would keep those promises, no matter the cost. Bowman and Hayes, with others on either side of the Mason-Dixon Line, reckoned Lincoln's ardent supporters failed to comprehend the overriding truth—a Union forged by war would never be strong. Welded seams would crack in the superheated hatred nurtured by succeeding generations of combatants.

Worse, slavery abolished by decree was an empty gesture, merely a sheet of paper bearing overblown language and signatures made elegant by the flourishes of a quill pen. Slavery, in one form or another, was as old as mankind. No signed decree changed that fact.

Bowman and Hayes agreed: The South would never pledge loyalty to the North. From Pennsylvania and Virginia to Alabama and Georgia, killing fields were soaked in blood. Seeds of disunity were sown deep in sacred ground, and everyone knew it.

Lincoln campaigners cited accounts of slavery—men branded, women bred like cows, runaways bloodied under the lash. Such volatile fuel inflamed Northerners on the eve of the election. Southern sympathizers countered with descriptive images of economic slavery among impoverished workers—downtrodden men, women, and children trapped in hell-hole factories while living in airless, disease-ridden tenements of the Northern industrial states.

McClellan was a man of reason, a gentleman willing to compromise, a West Pointer prepared to douse the fires of a war waged by brothers in arms. With a following among Republicans and a measure of adoration among the Northern citizenry, McClellan was the man of the hour.

But Atlanta fell, and more Union victories seemed imminent. Opinion was swayed. In the election Lincoln won 212 electoral votes to McClellan's 21. The popular vote told another tale. Out of a total of four million votes cast, Lincoln won by 400,000.

All hope was lost.

Roy took off his hat and wiped his brow. Since leaving Fairview, he had listened to Hayes give vent to his opinions and cite experiences of a lifetime. Lock this gent and Uncle Ab in the same room, Roy thought, and they will talk each other to death.

Hayes spoke of his service to General Grant and his steadfast friendship with A.P. Bowman. In the war, Hayes reminded him, Bowman was aide to the Confederate States of America's President Jefferson Davis.

Roy put on his hat. He knew of Bowman's rank and duties from John Nichols. Hayes's, too. He did not know both men had disliked their commanders. Grant was, according to Hayes, a "brutish lout", and Hayes quoted Bowman's description of Davis as "mad, raving mad."

Bowman and Hayes had that alienation in common, and more. Classmates at the Point, they had become close friends in the military academy. Later their friendship was secretly renewed in the war, and they continued an association through the tumultuous years of the nation rocked by insurrection.

Roy listened to Jay Dean Hayes's account of war and Sam Archer's lost love. Sober, Hayes was not only less combative than when he was stumbling drunk, he was downright talkative in an expansive way. In the telling, events of the past were separate strands woven into a tale as bizarre and vengeful as any Greek tragedy.

Roy had to admit Hayes's account of a wartime reunion with his old friend was compelling. The two generals had crossed trails at Salem Church outside Chancellorsville, meeting in the aftermath of a skirmish that proved to be a prelude to battle. During this period of tranquility before violence, they came from opposite directions on horseback, alone, raising a gloved hand when they recognized one another.

"For a moment back there," Bowman had said, reining up, "I believed I was going to have to kill you."

"My thought precisely, sir," Hayes had replied, deadpan, and shook Bowman's hand.

It made a bizarre scene, this churchyard where the combatants had fought and then withdrawn, leaving behind their dead. Bloodied corpses in blue uniforms had lain sprawled on the country lane while a dozen other lifeless figures dressed in gray or butternut had been piled against a rock fence as though strewn there by a deadly tide. The fence had enclosed a church cemetery where graves dated to the Revolution. In this place of silence and gore, the two opposing generals had shared a pint of bourbon while exchanging news of classmates' promotions and demotions, of death and injury in the high command.

All the while, Bowman had kept a watchful eye. Hayes had frequently looked over his shoulder, too. Fraternization was tantamount to spying, a war crime punishable by hanging. Yet A.P. Bowman and Jay Dean Hayes, their friendship renewed near a church cemetery where bodies lay above ground and below, had vowed to meet again.

From that day to the last hours of the war, they had met in secret, either in simple disguise or with uniforms covered by greatcoats or slickers. Over ale and supper in far-flung country taverns or in shaded clearings deep in a forest, they had discussed old times and new politics. They had found deep currents of agreement, particularly in the futility of this war. Assigned to traverse front lines, both had witnessed carnage. Both had been keenly aware men had died in agony by the thousands while Lincoln and Davis refused to negotiate terms for a truce.

Even though Bowman and Hayes had attained high rank in a short span of time, and although they reported to influential figures, they had been powerless to alter events. They had even considered desertion, and discussed where and how to escape the noose of military justice.

Then came an opportunity. Bowman grabbed it.

In tangible form, the "opportunity" had been minted gold and silver coins, sterling silver, cut diamonds, gleaming rubies, and blue sapphires—gems by the handful. Hayes had admitted that much to Roy now. He confirmed the scholar's research was accurate. John Nichols had been correct when he stated the infantry scout had seen a stolen treasure. Roy Smith had glimpsed it changing hands when he had observed two generals transferring saddlebags from one horse to the other on that last day of the war.

Hayes defended the act of theft. "Consider the circumstances," he said to Roy by way of *apologia,* and went on to recount events as Bowman had stated them.

During a night of fierce, wind-driven rains, A.P. Bowman had taken shelter in a glen. He had dismounted and hunkered down, soaked to the bone. While storm winds had lashed him, he invented an encounter with the captain of a British blockade runner. Later he had claimed to have boarded a two-masted brigantine in the port of Norfolk, leaping free when storm-tossed waves hit. That leap and the captain's last shouts over the roar of high winds had been dramatic—and fictional. In truth, Bowman had simply waited out the storm until morning. He kept the treasure for himself.

In the buggy seat now, Jay Dean Hayes had turned to Roy. "Under the circumstances, what else could he have done?"

"Told the truth," Roy said.

"To whom?"

"Reckon that's the question Bowman should have answered," Roy said. "He could have returned the gems and coins to the rightful owners."

"But how?" Hayes demanded. "No list existed. None of the donors had expected to get their gems and coins back, either."

Roy said: "He should have tried to return them."

"It is all too easy to look back and pass facile judgment," Hayes said. "All too easy."

Hayes went on to cite events that day Robert E. Lee rode Traveler to Appomattox Courthouse. Grant had waited there. The war had ended formally when the high-born gentleman surrendered to the son of a tanner.

Lee had sworn allegiance to the United States, and ordered all soldiers to do the same. By Lincoln's decree, there would be no hangings, no political prisoners taken. The war was over. Return home, Lee had said, and live in peace. Combatants were allowed to keep their weapons, but from here on firearms were to be used to feed families, not to kill fellow citizens. Five days later the President had been shot to death in Washington by a theater actor, gone mad.

In the aftermath, lawlessness coursed through the South like venom. With all the turmoil, Hayes claimed, Bowman could not have backtracked and admitted he held a treasure, even if he had wanted to. Word of it would only have invited fraud or robbery, or worse. Further complicating matters, Jefferson Davis himself had been at large, hunted by Yankees.

A.P. Bowman had been privy to the schemes and dreams of Jefferson Davis, and had resigned his commission after the surrender. Hayes simply had abandoned his. Bowman had known Davis planned to smuggle arms, supplies, and anything of value to Mexico. From there he would launch new attacks through Texas, commanding an army of zealots who refused to surrender to any Yankee, anywhere, any time.

Beyond his initial account of the storm, Bowman had never been interrogated about the fate of the treasure or the existence of a blockade runner no one else had seen. Bowman had decided to protect the treasure, withholding it from the clutches of a desperate, defeated President, or from bandits roaming the South like carrion-eaters.

Secrecy had been of utmost importance. He had confided only to his friend, Hayes. Fearing detection, Bowman had turned the treasure over to him. Hayes had discarded his uniform and gone into hiding for a time. At first, the plan had been no more elaborate than to protect the fortune and keep it intact. Someday it would be put to good use, exemplifying the values and traditions of the South.

While neither Bowman nor Hayes had favored the presidency of Abraham Lincoln, they did not countenance government by assassination, either. They had been shocked by the murder in a box in Ford's Theater—and filled with dread. Dire predictions of continued violence had consumed newspaper pages and energized tavern debates. A bloodbath had passed in four years, folks said, but another was coming—this one longer, bloodier.

Abraham Lincoln, the President who had prosecuted the war, could possibly have taken on the mantle of peacemaker had he lived. But the former Vice President, Andrew Johnson, had ascended to the office. Perceived as vindictive, Johnson had not been respected. True to form, he had ruled secessionist states with a heavy hand. He also had squandered money from the United States Treasury with the purchase of an ice-locked wasteland known as Alaska. He later escaped impeachment by one vote.

The large-scale war was over, folks had agreed, but elements were in place for a protracted guerrilla war. In all likelihood the war of insurrection would continue. Bands of Rebels would ambush Federal patrols. Bluecoats would in turn retaliate. Rebs would fade away like gray ghosts to attack another day. In the end the war-weary North would sue for peace, and the South would set the terms.

Whether such a scenario would ever play out or not, Bowman and Hayes had believed some form of perpetual warfare was at hand. There had been but one escape. Studying government maps, they had looked westward.

Beyond the far horizon lay mountain and plain, a vast region holding promise for a new beginning. The Western frontier offered refuge and renewal, not only for those who had lost everything in the war, but for those who had won and found victory to be hollow.

Bowman penned impassioned letters to Regina Stans. Receiving no answer, he visited her family's home in Petersburg. Among the ruins, the Stans' residence was a fine brick and stone house overlooking the mists of the Appomattox River.

The woman for whom Bowman had declared his love had refused to meet him alone. Her mother had stood by in the drawing room. Bowman, sporting tailor-made clothing and a diamond stickpin, had regaled Regina with extravagant promises for their future, claiming they were spiritually linked, destined to walk hand in hand for all time.

Bowman obliquely had referred to wealth and boasted of founding a great ranch out West where the values of the South would be honored. Just as the Parthenon had been built for Athena, how could Regina turn away from a life of luxury in a palace of her own?

"We are destined for greatness," he had said, "just as our forebears a century and a half ago founded the great plantations and built a civilization unrivaled in history."

Regina Stans had turned her back to him. She had not spoken, but had stood with her mother in the living room of a house still bearing the bitter odor of smoke from wartime flames. Mrs. Stans informed him that Mr. Stans had recently succumbed to gangrene, dying in agony from a war wound thought to be on the mend.

Mrs. Stans had invited the general to leave. Frustrated, Bowman had raised his voice, demanding Regina's attention. She had fled, hands to her face. Mrs. Stans moved to the front entrance and opened the door. She stood there, still and mute, until Bowman stomped out, hat in hand.

"A cruel jest from the classical era, isn't it," Bowman later had confided to Hayes.

"Jest?" Hayes had asked.

"Struck by Cupid's arrow," he had replied, "my judgment was clouded by desire. I behaved stupidly."

"But where is the jest?" Hayes had asked.

"Come now," Bowman had answered. "Can it be a coincidence that Cupid rhymes with stupid?"

Determined to pursue a new life after the war, he had adopted a new name. "Archer" came from the cherubic archer of legend, Cupid, the son of Venus. The name cleverly evoked "Bowman". "Sam" was a childhood nickname. Out West this tall, broad-shouldered gentleman would be known as "Sam Archer", cattle rancher and horse breeder of note, a man destined for greatness.

Armed with two pistols each, Sam Archer and Jay Dean Hayes had carried the treasure in money belts and a horsehide grip to New York City. In Manhattan they had converted gems and jewelry to cash in the American offices of the English firm, Carter's Emporium, Ltd., a respected gem broker. From there they had traveled to Pennsylvania by train, and on to Lancaster by private coach. Side curtains drawn, one of them had always been awake and alert for road agents.

Archer and Hayes had commissioned the construction of eight Conestoga wagons. A cash payment had assured completion of their special order in three weeks, record time. Rolling off the ramp, the sturdy vehicles were identical from tongue to tailgate—or so they had appeared. One was marginally different. The distinction between that Conestoga and seven others was a false bottom built into the wagon box. Under raised floorboards, a narrow space had been created, detectable only by the measure of a carpenter's rule or a wagon builder's critical eye.

Away from all eyes, Archer and Hayes had bundled greenbacks and had wrapped each one in oilcloth. They had packed them in canvas coin bags, and had concealed their cache of cash in the wagon's false bottom. Under their watchful gazes, the wagons had been shipped by rail, loaded with tools and supplies. Oxen had been purchased, teamsters hired. Ferried across the Mississippi River, they had joined a wagon train of forty-six settlers and fifteen gold seekers.

Beyond the jumping-off place in Missouri, a long, dusty trek lay ahead. In nine weeks Archer and Hayes had reached the southern sector of Wyoming Territory. From the Laramie town site, their eight covered wagons had veered off the emigrant trail.

Angling northward, Sam Archer had guided them with government maps. This land had been acquired from France by the Louisiana Purchase of 1803, and the terrain was still unexplored beyond blackened campfire rings left by surveyors. At last Archer and Hayes had come to a tent camp, a fledgling settlement called Fairview.

Encouraged by the lay of the land, Archer rode to the site

he had spotted on exploration maps. The presence of water was indicated, but until he saw Arapaho Creek, beaver ponds, and wetlands with his own eyes, he had been skeptical. After all, in common parlance the region was known as a desert.

Satisfied, he rode back to Laramie to buy land and register his Bar-A-Bar brand with the territorial government. At the Land Office a wide-eyed clerk had pushed his visor up on his forehead and stared at stacks of the cash before him. This stranger, Samuel Archer, had walked in the door with enough greenbacks to choke a horse. Archer had paid for the land as well as for water and mineral rights. With the stroke of a pen, he had taken ownership of property known from that day on as the Bar-A-Bar Ranch.

In recounting the past, Hayes filled in one last blank. Cupid's arrow was deeply imbedded. Archer had pined for Regina Stans. He wished he had presented himself in a gentlemanly way, a manner above reproach. He wished he had won over the mother before approaching the daughter. He wished he had been acquainted with the father. He wished. . . .

Troubling regrets had filled his mind. In his misery, he had penned love letters to Regina, but never posted them. Instead, he threw himself into his work. To build his ranch, Sam Archer had purchased cattle and horses, as well as materials and the services of craftsmen. He had hired cowhands, paying top wages in the territory at $3.50 a day, bed and board included. That first summer season building materials had been freighted to the ranch. Tradesmen had come the next summer, and built the house. Bunkhouses, horse barns, outbuildings, and pole corrals had been constructed later. Everything that did not move had been painted white. The Bar-A-Bar was the most impressive cattle ranch in the territory.

Like the supernatural forces of darkness, storm clouds darkened the sun, bringing inevitable doom to Greek players. For Sam Archer, it was the day the last of the fortune had been spent, the day every last coin and greenback were gone.

Hayes had offered loans, meager as they were, knowing Archer would decline. In Fairview, Hayes lived alone in a modest clapboard house, supported by revenues from his purchase of Stubbs's livery and interest on loans to Frankie over the years.

Sam Archer was still a man of some wealth. His land holdings were owned free and clear, his cattle and horse herds numerous. He lived in his ranch house in comfort, albeit alone.

With no cash reserve, Archer had faced the same narrow margin of survival nature meted out to other Wyoming stockmen. Depending on the price of beef in distant stockyards and depending on the vagaries of a climate ranging from winter blizzards to summer droughts, some years had been bountiful, others disastrous. The march of years had taken their toll upon Archer, too, leaving the man dependent on his ranch foreman to turn a profit.

Over the years other cattle ranches had been established in Buffalo County. Added to them, lone homesteaders made their way to creeks and water holes. The newcomers pitched tents and lived out of their wagons until cabins were built. In ill-advised experiments some nesters had attempted to plow ground, learning the hard way that this dry earth would not support a marketable crop. Prairie winds swirled dust skyward from these failed attempts, and spring rain sent rivulets of mud slithering away from farms, leaving patches of bare dirt and exposed rocks on the landscape.

Virtually every settler in the region had clung to a belief that the Union Pacific Railroad would run steel to Fairview.

Their future would be assured when that first locomotive steamed across the prairie to the Wyoming settlement, whistle blowing, the stack belching black coal smoke into a blue sky.

Time had proved them wrong.

Roy drove the buggy downslope from the rim overlooking Bar-A-Bar headquarters. The door to the root cellar caught his eye. Despite the heat, a chill climbed his spine. The door to the cellar was closed now, but the memory of dark, airless isolation was vivid in his mind, a memory of suffocation closing around him.

Roy guided the team to the portico of the Bar-A-Bar ranch house and halted. The front door swung open. Archer came out. He tugged at the lapels of his high-waisted coat, straightening the black garment as he prepared himself to receive guests. He gimped across the portico to greet his old friend, but drew up when he recognized Roy on the buggy seat beside Hayes.

Arm thrust out, a gnarled index finger jabbed at Roy. "Get off my land."

Roy hauled back on the lines. He gazed at the old general. Behind the bent figure, leaded glass windows caught the midday sunlight like cut diamonds. Archer halted between two fluted columns. The columns supported a peaked roof over the porch, and once again Roy noted paint peeling from wood shaped to imitate marble.

He remembered first impressions upon entering the mansion—a cavernous interior downstairs and empty rooms with cobwebbed corners and dust-covered floors upstairs. Now when he looked at this imposing structure, he did not see a mansion on the prairie. He saw an old man's dreams, empty and dusty, too.

"Mister, I won't tell you again."

"We heard you, Sam, we heard you." Hayes spoke as he swung his thick body around. With a grunt, he stepped down from the carriage seat. He beckoned to Roy, and went on talking to Archer.

"After we settle a matter, this gent will leave Buffalo County." Hayes glanced at Roy for confirmation. "Won't you?"

When Roy offered no reply, Archer uttered a curse.

"Where is John Nichols?" Roy demanded. Met by silence, he went on: "I figure you know. That's why you tried to kill me."

"Kill you?"

"You shoved me into that cellar at gunpoint," Roy reminded him.

"Son," Archer said, "if I'd meant to kill you, you wouldn't be standing here now, stinking up the place." Archer turned to Hayes. "I won't stand for his interrogations."

"Sam, we'll go over it one last time," Hayes said, "and I'll escort Mister Smith off the ranch. In Fairview, I'll send him packing."

The rancher shook his head, but offered no further objection when Roy left the buggy and looped the lines around a tie post. Mounting the steps behind Hayes, Roy followed him across the portico. They entered the great room after Archer. He led the way into his library while Hayes slapped powdery dust from his suit.

"Fact is, Sam," Hayes said, "we both have a thirst and a hunger. Fetch us a tumbler of water and a double shot of your finest. Have Cookie rustle up some chow."

"That girl isn't here to fetch drinks or dinner or anything else," Archer said. He pointed at Roy. "She ran off with him. Cookie saw them."

"Yes, yes," Hayes said. "I spoke to Martha. She refuses to live on the ranch a day longer. She's determined to go to Laramie. Mister Smith will take her there, I hear."

Archer turned to face Roy and squared his shoulders. "She is not a respectable woman."

Roy eyed him. "She gave birth to your son."

"She's lying about that," Archer said.

"How do you know?" Roy asked.

Obviously not a man accustomed to being questioned, Archer stiffened. "The equation is simple. Of the men she takes in that crib, I possess the greatest wealth. Thus, she claims I fathered her baby." He added: "She won't get any money. Not from me."

"Martha will find it difficult to walk away from Frankie," Hayes observed. "The old bat does not let go of her girls easily. It's business."

"Either way, she's no longer here," Archer said.

"True enough," Hayes agreed as though discussing the weather.

"I made do before she came," Archer went on, "and I'll make do now that she's gone. If you want a meal, you'll have to hike down to the cook shack and tell Cookie yourself."

Deadpan, Hayes asked: "Will he make us wait until the hands ride in?"

Archer nodded. "Likely so."

"Cookie runs this ranch," Hayes said with a smile.

Obviously a point of humor between them, Archer did not pick up on the familiar joke in the presence of a stranger.

"Supper can wait, I suppose," Hayes said. He stood. "I will pour a libation."

Roy watched the fat man cross the library to a stoneware crock on an oak stand. Removing the lid, he ladled branch water into three glass tumblers. Then he opened a cabinet and brought out a long-necked bottle, squinting as he examined the label. He nodded approval, pulled the cork, and poured generous double shots.

Roy watched Hayes lift his shot glass and look pensively at the amber liquor as though regarding an old friend. He handed one to Roy, the other to Archer. They drank in silence until the rancher spoke up.

"I've got nothing to say to this man."

Roy said: "Bowman, I had you in my gunsights."

Startled by that name and that claim, Archer flinched. "What do you mean?"

"You were a dead man," Roy answered, "until I took my finger off the trigger of my Springfield."

Archer turned to Hayes. "What is he raving on about?"

"Listen to him, Sam," Hayes said quietly. "He knows the truth."

Archer swore. "He's got you believing that?"

"Hear him out," Hayes repeated, and nodded at Roy.

Roy recounted events he had described to Hayes, relating details in that last day of the war. When he finished, Archer disputed his account. He denied ever committing a crime. He was the armed guardian of a treasure later lost at sea.

Roy heard a stubborn tone in that deep voice. High and mighty as he was, Roy knew Archer would neither defend nor explain his actions. Taking a page from Uncle Ab's book, Roy argued the point with an aphorism. "A thief is the feller who never returns property that doesn't belong to him."

Face flushed, Archer sputtered in a rush of anger.

Roy went on: "John Nichols read your letters to a woman named Regina Stans. You bragged of wealth, and she turned her back on you. That was when you decided to go out West and build this ranch with a stolen fortune."

With that, Sam Archer ordered him off his property.

Following wagon wheel ruts across the plain away from the Bar-A-Bar, Roy felt pangs of hunger. He and Hayes had left the ranch without supper, and now he glanced at the fat man. Hayes was silent. Roy figured the man's mind was occupied by the argument that had flared in Archer's library.

His gaze was drawn to a blur of movement. In the sage one hundred yards off to his left, he saw coyotes leaping, eight or ten of them frolicking as they yipped and growled at one another. Overhead, small birds darted out of the sky. Roy hauled back on the lines.

"What's wrong?" Hayes asked.

Roy pointed to the coyotes. "They usually don't bunch up until late autumn. When the weather turns cold, they hunt in packs. They aim to bring down as much game as they can before the snow flies. That's how they get through the winters."

Hayes looked at the coyotes, and turned to Roy. "What are you driving at?"

When he did not answer immediately, Hayes repeated his question.

"Carrion, likely," Roy replied. "Some kind of easy prey is drawing coyotes over there. Whatever it is, I figure it's dead."

He set the brake and stepped down from the buggy seat. Striding through knee-high sage and yellow-flowering rabbitbrush toward the pack of coyotes, a stench of rotting flesh came to him. Hand to his mouth, he slowed, glad his stomach was empty.

Several coyotes fled when he drew near. The more aggressive adults hunkered down, baring teeth as they faced a two-legged intruder. Scrawny as runaway dogs, their splotched gray-brown coats effectively camouflaged them. One coyote snarled, but beat a retreat when Roy drew closer and slapped his hands together. The others followed.

Roy spotted one last coyote. He saw a gnawed bone in its jaws. Roy moved close enough to see the twitching nose on a pointed snout. Still growling, the predator seemed unwilling to relinquish his food without a fight.

Roy took off his hat and waved it. Spooked, the coyote turned and loped away, dropping the gnawed bone. Roy moved closer. On the ground he saw a forearm with shriveled skin, small bones broken at the wrist of a human hand.

Roy had sensed what he would find here. Even so, the shock of discovery hit him hard. That, and the pervasive stench made him nauseous and light-headed. Hurrying on, he saw scattered bones and gray flesh. In a shallow ravine he spotted the remains of two dead horses, matched blacks. They bore the brand of Harvey Baker's livery.

Beyond the carcasses, Roy saw fabric on the ground. He stepped closer and found a light canvas duster. Animals had clawed and tugged at the fabric. Even though torn, Roy knew it was a garment identical to the one he had seen John Nichols wearing. He knelt. Reaching out, he pulled fabric away from the corpse. He exposed the stilled face of a round-cheeked man with reddish hair, the jaw and neck peppered by a shotgun blast. Judging by a tight pattern, the weapon had been fired at close range.

# Chapter Nine

Roy heard a muffled curse. The subdued voice came from behind him. Standing, he turned to find Jay Dean Hayes approaching. The fat man swore under his breath again as his gaze fell upon human remains on the ground. "Nichols?" Hayes asked, halting.

Roy nodded.

"Good Lord," he said.

Both men stood in reverential silence. At last Hayes lifted his gaze to Roy.

"I know you do not hold Sam in high regard," he said, "or me, either, for that matter. But I assure you, neither one of us had a hand in this murder."

"How do you know Archer didn't?" Roy asked.

"As I informed you in Bess and Jimmy's place," Hayes replied, "Sam doesn't operate that way. Neither do I. We saw too much of it in the war." Hayes studied him. "I believe you did, too."

They stood in silence until Hayes offered a confession. "I drink to forget. What do you do?"

Roy thought about that. "Work."

"Every man to his poison," Hayes said.

Roy changed the subject. "What about Brennan and Dwyer?"

"What about them?" Hayes asked.

"They're a pair of hardcases."

"I would not disagree with that characterization," Hayes said. "Sam runs his ranch in the best way he knows how.

Riding herd on livestock is only part of the job. It takes a certain type of man to ride herd on cowhands. Some cowhands will rob a rancher blind. Just as a planter requires the services of an overseer, a rancher needs a foreman. The Bar-A-Bar is a big spread. Sam hired two tough men to get the job done."

"If Archer told Brennan and Dwyer to gun down a trespasser," Roy asked, "they'd follow orders, wouldn't they?"

"Preposterous," Hayes said. He looked down at the human remains again. "Sam wouldn't kill a man. Not this way."

"What way would he?" Roy asked.

Hayes considered his answer. "Self-defense, I suppose. Same as any other man would."

"If Nichols showed up at his ranch," Roy said, "demanding money in a swap for keeping quiet about a stolen Confederate treasure, Sam Archer just might take that as a threat to his life."

"You're forgetting one thing," Hayes said.

"What's that?"

"It's gone, all of it," Hayes replied. "The last gold eagle was spent a long time ago. With it went proof that a treasure ever existed."

"Maybe Nichols didn't believe that," Roy said. "Or maybe he figured Archer could raise cash by selling off some steers . . . enough to keep him from riding to the federal marshal's office in Cheyenne to report a war crime."

Hayes studied him. "Maybe. But where does that leave us now?"

Roy looked at the gnawed bones and sun-dried flesh pulled away from clothing by the sharp teeth of animals. "It leaves us with a man shot to death, gunned down and left here on the prairie to rot."

Hayes eyed him. "What do you plan to do?"

"Go back to Bar-A-Bar headquarters," Roy said.

"For what purpose?" Hayes asked.

"To tell Archer that John Nichols is on his property," Roy replied.

Roy had little doubt that if Hayes had not been at his side, Archer would have been provoked to commit murder. The rancher met them on the portico, his face flushed, eyes fixed on Roy.

"What the hell are you doing back here?" Archer demanded.

Roy saw the man's knees buckle, and wondered if anger had sapped his strength after their argument, or if the old man had slugged down too many double shots of Kentucky bourbon. Like a drunken dancer, Archer half pirouetted and wrapped his arms around a white column. He slowly slid to the plank flooring and sat there, gray head lolling.

"Sam!" Hayes yelled, mounting the steps in his heavy and awkward stride. "Sam!"

"Get . . . get thash man offen mah propitty," Archer said, his words slurring.

Hayes nodded at Roy. Despite protests, the two of them brought Archer to his feet. They steadied him and took him inside to a settee in the library. He stretched out. His face pale now, he was still enraged by the presence of Roy Smith.

Roy glanced around the paneled room. The long-necked bottle stood on a side table by the liquor cabinet, uncorked and empty.

"Run him . . . run him offen mah proppity," Archer repeated.

"I will," Hayes replied. He paused. "Sam, we found the body."

Archer raised his head. "Body?"

"The body of John Nichols," Hayes said. "We found him a few miles from here, along with the carcasses of two matched blacks. Whoever committed the crime, shot the horses, too."

Archer sank back on the upholstered settee.

"Who killed Nichols?" Roy demanded.

"Get . . . get out."

"I'll get out," Roy said, "when you start telling the truth."

Archer summoned enough strength to level another curse at him, but in the next moment his eyes closed and he passed out, snoring.

Hayes pulled back.

Roy said: "I'm not leaving until I get an answer. . . ."

He was interrupted by drumming hoof beats, rhythmic sounds drifting through the front doorway. Remembering the door to the great room stood open, Roy moved hurriedly to a leaded glass window.

He saw two riders rein up beside the buggy. One was Buck Brennan. The second horseman was Mike Dwyer. Both men swung down and tied their mounts. They exchanged a glance before turning toward the portico steps.

"Wait here," Roy said to Hayes.

Drawing his revolver, he left the library. He eased into the great room and stepped behind the open door. Presently the sounds of ringing spur rowels and booted footfalls reached him. A shadow stretched across the floor in the entryway, and then came a second one.

"Mister Archer?" Brennan called out. He ventured in, followed by Dwyer. "Mister Archer?"

Roy gave the door a shove. It slammed shut. Brennan stiffened. Dwyer halted in his tracks. Roy stepped out as both men spun around, surprise registering in their faces. Anger replaced amazement when Roy leveled his gun at them at point-blank range.

"Drop your gun belts," Roy said. His gaze took in Dwyer. "Both of you."

Brennan swore.

"Do as I say . . . now."

Brennan seemed ready to defy him. Dwyer followed the foreman's lead, his hand inching toward the grips of his holstered handgun.

"You won't get both of us," Brennan said.

"I'll get you," Roy said to him.

Brennan blinked, but made no move.

Roy stepped back a pace. He pointed the revolver upward and pulled the trigger. The loud report startled both men. Amid gunpowder smoke, the bullet brought down a shower of fine white plaster from the ceiling. Roy aimed the Colt at Brennan.

"The next one is for you," Roy said, and thumbed the hammer back.

Both men hastily unbuckled their gun belts, letting holstered sidearms slide to the floor.

"You're gonna regret this," Brennan muttered.

"One of us will," Roy said. He asked: "Why did you kill him?"

"Who?"

"John Nichols."

"The city man?" Brennan said. "Hell, I didn't kill him."

Roy shifted the gun, bringing the business end to bear on Dwyer. "Must have been you, then."

"I didn't kill nobody," the smaller man said, his voice cracking.

Roy said: "I figure you two followed orders from Archer. . . ."

Dwyer cut him off. "Damn it, I never killed nobody."

"Then why did you two gents hide the Dunston carriage in

Stubbs's livery barn?" Roy asked.

"We found that rig in a ravine," Brennan explained. "Wasn't no sign of the city man. Or a team, either. We towed the Dunston into Fairview. Told Stubbs to keep it until the owner showed up."

"We took it to pieces," Dwyer said, "so it wouldn't be in his way."

"Mighty thoughtful of you good citizens," Roy allowed. "Reckon you covered it up with a pile of wagon covers to keep the barn dust off it."

Angered by the sarcasm, Dwyer cursed Roy. Brennan glowered.

"You two stole that carriage," Roy went on, "after you killed Nichols. I figure you shot the horses because stealing matched blacks branded from a livery barn is a risky business."

"You can't prove nothing," Brennan said.

Dwyer chimed in: "If that city man's dead, I've got a pretty good notion who done it." He pointed to Roy. "Tom Hood."

Before Roy could deny the accusation, a voice came from the library.

"This man is not Tom Hood."

In a sidelong glance, Roy saw Hayes step out of the library.

"You sure?" Dwyer asked him.

Hayes nodded. "I'm certain."

Dwyer held to his story. "Must have been a dry-gulcher who done the killing."

Brennan added: "Hood's a lone wolf. Paid in advance. Fires long range from ambush. He leaves the dead man's head resting on a stone, I heard."

"He rides out," Dwyer added. "Nobody knows where he goes."

Roy heard a rehearsed tone in their voices. He figured the pair had concocted this tale. It might have sounded plausible when they went over it alone on the range, but here the words rang hollow.

"Just who do you figure hired Hood?" Roy asked.

"We'll never know," Brennan said. "The man operates in secret."

Dwyer added: "Sometimes he don't even know hisself who paid him. That's what I heard."

"Handy for the yarn you're spinning, isn't it?" Roy said.

"You can't prove nothing different," Dwyer insisted.

Brennan said to Roy: "You'd be smart to put that gun away and ride."

"While you're able," Dwyer added.

"Tough talk," Roy said, swinging the Colt toward him.

Dwyer's gaze narrowed. "I can back it up. Put your gun down. We'll go at it, man to man."

Roy jerked his head toward Brennan. "Last time I faced you, he sucker-punched me. It won't happen again."

"What do you aim to do?" Brennan asked.

"You're going into that root cellar," Roy said to him, "where you put me."

A look of fear crossed Brennan's face. "You can't do that."

Now Roy leveled his gun at him. "Want to take a bullet instead?"

Brennan swallowed. "You've got nothing to fear from us."

"Glad to hear that," Roy said. "Question is, what do you have to fear from me?"

Hayes had been watching their dispute unfold. He advanced a pace. "Just what do you plan to do, Mister Smith?"

"The right thing," he replied.

"By your lights," Hayes asked, "what is the right thing?"

"John Nichols deserves proper burying and a marker,"

Roy answered. "I'll see that he gets both. Where, depends on the wishes of his widow."

Hayes eyed him. "Then will you travel by rail to Cheyenne?"

"Why would I do that?"

"To send U.S. marshals into Buffalo County," Hayes replied. "That's your line of thinking, isn't it?"

"On the home place I aim to tend my livestock and catch up on chores," Roy said. "That's my line of thinking." He turned to Buck Brennan. "Move."

"Being closed in don't suit me . . . ," Brennan stammered. "It just don't. I'm asking you, Smith. Don't put me in that cellar. . . ." He drew a ragged breath. "I never aimed to leave you in there . . . not for long."

"That's a comfort," Roy said.

"I know you don't believe me, but. . . ." Brennan's voice trailed off.

"With no air in there," Roy broke in, "a man could take his last breath in the dark."

Brennan's gaze was fixed on Roy.

"Ever wonder what it feels like to be buried alive?" Roy asked. "Hell of a feeling. Hollering doesn't help. You can shout all you want . . . except you wouldn't want to waste your breath, would you?"

Seeing abject fear in the man's face, Roy led him on, figuring it was good medicine for a bully. "It's dead quiet down there, Brennan. Dead quiet. Dark as a cave. Nothing but dead air to breathe. The dark closes in like a weight shoving down on your chest. . . ."

"I only done what Mister Archer ordered me to do," Brennan broke in. "I'd have set you loose as soon as I could . . . that's the honest truth."

"Honest truth," Roy repeated.

Seeing a look of distress etched into the foreman's face, Roy tried to give him the impression he was taking new testimony into consideration.

"Want me to let you off the hook, Buck?"

"Huh?" Brennan said in surprise.

"Don't get me wrong," Roy said. "You're headed for that cellar. But. . . ."

"But what?" Brennan asked. "You're not making sense."

Roy jerked his head toward Dwyer. "Your *segundo* will let you out after he finishes a chore."

"Chore?" Dwyer demanded. "Now what are you talking about?"

Roy turned to him. "I'll drive the buggy on the Fairview Road while you walk ahead of the team."

"Walk?" Dwyer asked in disbelief. "All the way to town?"

Roy shook his head. "To the gulch where we found the remains of John Nichols."

"What the hell for?" Dwyer demanded.

"Like I said," Roy answered, "there's a chore to be done."

"Chore? What chore?"

"Wrap the body in his duster," Roy explained, "and load it into the back of the buggy. Then you'll hike back here to the ranch house while Mister Hayes and I head for Fairview."

Dwyer shook his head slowly. "I won't touch a dead man. No, sir."

"You'll touch this one," Roy said.

Dwyer shook his head again in a stubborn gesture of defiance.

Roy leveled the Colt, aiming below the waist. "Reckon this takes us back to a bullet. Want me to leave you here with a bullet through you, squirming and hollering while you're bleeding like a stuck pig?"

The foreman and his *segundo* exchanged glances again,

both men angered and at once desperate for a way to gain the upper hand. Roy figured they meant to take him down. He stepped back, bringing Mister Colt's equalizer to bear on them.

"Outside, gents," Roy said. "Move. I aim to be in Fairview before dark."

Dwyer stared at him, jaw clenched. So did Brennan. After a long moment they exchanged a glance and turned. They walked out the door. Roy left the great room and descended the portico steps behind them. Hayes followed.

At the tie post, Roy ordered Brennan and Dwyer to halt. Roy trained his gun on them as he went to their horses and opened the saddlebags. Thrusting his hand into one, he pulled out a running iron. In another he found a cut-down shotgun. The double barrels had been shortened to twelve inches, the stock sawed off at the pistol grip.

Roy lifted the weapon, broke it open, and sniffed at the breech. A bitter scent of burned gunpowder filled his nostrils.

"Yours, Dwyer?" Roy asked.

"That's my varmint gun," he replied. "I use it on rattlers and such."

"You tried to use it on me," Roy said.

"Huh?"

"After you kicked in the door to Bess and Jimmy's cabin," Roy reminded him.

"The hell I did," Dwyer said.

Roy thrust the shotgun back into the saddlebag, and motioned with the Colt. "Move."

At gunpoint he marched them to the cellar. Hayes looked on in silence while Roy ordered Dwyer to lift the heavy door. The *segundo* hesitated.

"You want to go down there, too?" Roy asked.

Dwyer did not move for a moment. Then, avoiding

Brennan's hard-eyed gaze, he did as he was told and lifted the heavy door.

"Damn you," Brennan said softly.

Roy motioned to Brennan. "Get in there. Go on. Soon as Dwyer gets back from his chore, you'll get a breath of fresh air."

When the big man hesitated, Roy reminded him: "You shoved me in there at gunpoint, Brennan. Now it's your turn. Take it like a man."

Jaw clenched, Brennan cast a look of anger at him. He peered down into the cellar as though eyeing his own grave. Then he took one hesitant step.

"Hurry it up," Roy said.

Brennan slowly descended the stairs. When he reached the bottom, Roy motioned to Dwyer.

The *segundo* let the door fall shut. Roy leaned away from a gust of dust rising into the air. Then he bent down and shoved the deadbolt home.

"Come on," Roy said to Dwyer.

Uncle Ab had been right, Roy thought, when he had said: "No critter on the face of the earth hates to be set afoot more than a cowhand hates it. Walking does not suit a man accustomed to a commandin' view of the world from the saddle. Walking! Walking is for farmers. Walking is for miners."

Roy forced Dwyer to walk. From the buggy seat he saw the man's neck bowed in anger as he trudged along wheel ruts ahead of the team of horses. Jay Dean Hayes occupied two-thirds of the seat beside him. For once the fat man had nothing to say.

At first Dwyer cast hard looks over his shoulder to show his anger. After cresting the rise overlooking the ranch head-quarters behind them, he strode onward, each step in boots with pointed toes and heels meant for the stirrup. After the first half mile the man was footsore. He walked gimpily, shoulders dipping and pitching with every step.

When Roy saw a dark cloud of blackbirds in the sky, he called out directions to Dwyer. They angled off the road, spooking coyotes. The stench of rotting flesh drifted to them; Dwyer gagged. Clapping a hand over his mouth and nose, the man spun around. He swore, and renewed his objections to performing this task Roy had forced on him.

"This ain't no damned chore! I ain't gonna do it!"

Roy raised the Colt. "You might want to give that some thought."

A long moment passed while Roy drew aim. With a curse, Dwyer yanked a bandanna from his hip pocket. Covering his mouth and nose, he knotted the fabric at the back of his neck. He roundly cursed Roy again for putting him through such misery and humiliation under the gun.

"The sooner you get the job done," Roy said, "the sooner you'll hike back to the ranch house."

Dwyer protested, but finally complied. He gingerly gathered human body parts, lifted the torso and legs, and placed them on the duster. He gagged again. Turning away, he braced his hands on his knees and retched in dry heaves. When he refused to do any more of this grisly work, Roy cocked the revolver.

"I don't want to wing you, Dwyer," he said. "But if I have to, I will."

Once again, Mike Dwyer stood still. Roy wondered if he could shoot an unarmed man, even to wound him. Men died from bullet wounds, even minor wounds. Maybe Hayes had been right when he speculated Roy had seen too much carnage in the war to inflict violence on anyone now.

The moment passed. Roy's expression must have masked

that shadow of a doubt for Dwyer returned to the task. Finished at last, Roy helped him fold the canvas material over the remains of John Nichols. The two of them lifted and loaded the awkward bundle into the buggy, placing it behind the seat in a space meant for luggage.

Roy faced Dwyer. Despite the circumstances, he held back a smile. Some sight it was. With a bandanna covering the lower half of a face white as a sheet, Dwyer looked like an unarmed bandit, and a weak one at that.

Roy said now: "Pull off your boots."

"My boots?" Dwyer asked.

"Take them off."

"What the hell are you talking about . . . ?"

Roy swiftly aimed the Colt and snapped off a quick shot. The bullet plowed dirt and raised a dust cloud between his feet. The team of horses pranced. Hayes grabbed the lines.

"I'm talking about you taking orders," Roy said. "Now, pull off your boots."

"Why?"

"Why do you think?" Roy asked. "You're walking back to the ranch in your socks."

Dwyer cursed him.

"Pick up your boots next time you're in town," Roy said. "I'll leave them in the livery with Stubbs."

Dwyer stood still, too angry to spit. "Bastard."

"Don't go getting me riled," Roy warned him.

Jaw set, Dwyer scowled. "You bastard."

"Get me riled," Roy said, "and I'll send you back to the bunkhouse naked as the day you were born."

Eyeing the Colt, Dwyer grudgingly complied. He pulled off one boot and then the other, uncovering socks with holed-out toes and heels. Roy sent him on his way. He watched the *segundo* step gingerly through pear cactus and walk around clumps of sage as he made his way to the ranch road.

Roy picked up Dwyer's manured boots and tossed them under the seat of the buggy. Climbing up, he took the lines from Hayes. He turned the vehicle and drove toward the rutted ranch road leading to Fairview. He saw Hayes look back.

Roy glanced over his shoulder. Dwyer walked slowly, picking his way across the prairie like a man treading barefoot on broken glass.

"You've made two enemies," Hayes observed. "Brennan and Dwyer."

"Three," Roy corrected him, "counting Archer."

Roy had planned to sleep under the stars. He had misgivings about spending another night in Bess and Jimmy's cabin, despite their offer of free beer and pickled pigs' feet at their bar. Bess told him the cabin had been thoroughly cleaned and furnished with a new wool blanket and a feather pillow with a clean pillowslip. That was not all. Jimmy had rebuilt the door. He had installed steel hinges with an inside latch purchased at the mercantile.

"You'll be safe in there," Bess assured him.

Even though the attack last night was none of their doing, Roy knew Bess and Jimmy felt a measure of responsibility for it. They wanted to make amends.

He relented. If his attackers were Brennan and Dwyer, as he suspected, he figured the pair would find another way to come after him. All he could do now was watch his back. With thoughts of violence filling his mind, he drifted off to sleep. He was awakened late in the night by a tap on the door.

Roy's hand stabbed into darkness, fingers touching cold steel. He fumbled for his Colt. Finding the grips, his hand closed around them. He thumbed back the hammer and rolled out of the bunk.

He padded to the door in bare feet. Finger on the trigger, he unhooked the door latch with his free hand. He stepped aside. Opening the door, he leveled the revolver at his visitor. By starlight he saw a slight figure in a hooded cape reaching to slender ankles.

"Roy."

# Chapter Ten

Holding her baby, Martha O'Meara looked up at Roy by the dim light of stars. "J.D., he says you don't scare."

At his invitation she entered. While he lit the lamp and adjusted the wick, she told him she had come from Frankie's cabin. She had heard Jay Dean Hayes's account of their long day's journey from Fairview to the Bar-A-Bar Ranch headquarters, and back again.

Roy closed the cabin door. He pulled out the chair for her. When he sat on the bunk, they faced one another.

Martha went on: "J.D., he says you brung in the body of that city man. Says you and Mister Stubbs hammered up a coffin down at the livery."

Roy nodded. The makeshift coffin had been fashioned from wood available to them—ash boards pried off the broken-down Conestogas, buckboards, and mud wagons scattered in the weeds behind the barn. The coffin was held together with rusted nails, and covered with sun-bleached canvas. Not much to look at, it served the purpose, shroud and all.

In the barn Roy had helped Stubbs reassemble the Dunston. While working by the light of lanterns in the runway, Stubbs had inquired about the lay of the land in northern Colorado and the terrain of the Hat Creek basin in particular. Roy had described the L-Bar-7 and Box R ranches. He had mentioned the injury to his uncle, accounting for his eagerness to return to his home place.

Finished, Roy had left the barn and walked the length of

the street. He had stopped in at Bess and Jimmy's place for supper. That was when Bess had informed him of improvements made to the cabin, and offered a night's stay, no charge.

"Frankie," Martha went on now, "she says a girl like me won't never know the love of a man. Not true love from a good man. Soon as folks find out I done worked in the cribs, no man will love me. That's what Frankie says. Men use women like me to satisfy their urges. That's all it is, she says. Just urges. Maybe she's right. Mister Archer, he never treated me no better than a crib whore. Times, he took the belt to me to make me mind. Said I wasn't no lady." She added pensively: "What do you think?"

"About what?" Roy said.

He did not tell her he was recalling a remark he had overheard from Jay Dean Hayes to Sam Archer—*Martha will find it difficult to walk away from Frankie. The old bat does not let go of her girls easily. It's business.* Now Roy figured the madam was trying to scare Martha out of going to Laramie.

"About a man showing love," Martha replied. "True love. To a girl like me."

At a loss for words, Roy gazed at her. He saw a young, smooth-cheeked face in the glow of lamplight, eyes full of hope. He figured she wanted an answer that offered promise.

"Reckon there's men out there," he said, speaking slowly as he searched for the right words. "Plenty of men who want a good woman like you."

Martha eyed him. "That's just it. Frankie, she says I'm not a good woman. Says I never will be because I worked in the cribs. That's what I'm asking you about."

"You're pretty," Roy said. He looked at her, trying to think of something else to say. "And you dress nice. I figure, well, I figure there's plenty of men in Laramie who will want to get acquainted with you."

"Not just greasy railroaders?"

Roy shook his head. "There's plenty of other men in that town. . . ." His voice trailed off. He did not know what else to say. He wished Uncle Abner was here to take over. With Ab in the room, there was never any danger of awkward silences hanging in the air like leaden clouds.

"Roy," she said.

"What?"

"I still aim to go to Laramie," she said. "You still need someone to drive that high-wheeled buggy, don't you?"

He nodded. "If I can get hold of a team."

"Maybe we can borrow harness-broke horses from Stubbs's livery. . . ." Interrupted when the baby fussed, she rocked him gently.

Roy shook his head at her suggestion. "I'm leaving Fairview on a one-way road."

"One-way road?" she asked. "What do you mean by that?"

"When I leave this place," he replied, "I won't come back, not to return borrowed horses or anything else. The road I'm taking is one way from here to home."

Martha laughed suddenly. "Me, too, Roy. I'm leaving this burg on a one-way road, one way from here to Laramie."

Roy grinned. He had never heard her laugh before, and was surprised by the light, musical lilt. With the baby fussing again, she stood and shifted him to her hip.

"One thing keeps a-troubling me," she said.

"What?"

"Ever since J.D. told Frankie and me about you finding the body of Mister John Nichols out there on the prairie," she said, "well, I just keep a-wondering who killed him. Who done such a horrible thing? Reckon we'll ever know?"

"I don't know," Roy said.

"You think somebody around here done it?" she asked. "Or did he get dry-gulched by some stranger . . . dry-gulched and robbed?"

Roy said again: "I don't know."

"I just keep a-wondering," she mused. Her baby cried louder, and she moved to the door. "My Sam, he's hungry. Reckon I'd better do something about that."

Roy stood and opened the door for her. "I'll walk you to Frankie's."

"You don't have to do that," she said. "I walked over here by myself."

Roy recalled an observation by his mother long ago: A gentleman walks a lady to her door. Now he spoke over the insistent cries of the baby.

"A gentleman walks a lady to her door."

She looked at him and murmured: "Thank you."

Roy saw her smile by starlight. He took her arm. They made their way along the footpath and crossed the rutted street.

Roy returned from Frankie's cabin and blew out the lamp. He pulled off his boots and stretched out on the bunk, head resting on a clean and soft pillow. In truth, he had been plagued by the same question that troubled Martha. His anxiety mounted when he thought ahead. He would see Anne and her children at the home place. What would he tell them?

Roy had not ventured any of his theories to Martha, but he figured Buck Brennan and Mike Dwyer had committed the crime. He also believed they had tried to gun him down in the cabin. He could not prove either theory, just as he had no proof Sam Archer knew more than he had admitted. For that matter, Hayes probably knew more than he had acknowledged, too. Ever since the war years, secrecy had been the hallmark of their friendship.

Roy figured he was not the man to pry the truth out of them. As outlined by Uncle Ab, he had completed his task here. He was eager to ride, keen to put it all behind him—the Bar-A-Bar Ranch, Fairview, Buffalo County—all of it. The sooner he swung into the saddle, the sooner he would get home and catch up on L-Bar-7 chores.

After sunrise he took breakfast in Bess and Jimmy's place. While sawing a thick slice of ham with a dull knife, he heard the door open.

Stubbs entered. Glancing around the empty establishment, the liveryman marched to Roy's table. He stood before him, hat in hand.

" 'Morning," Roy said.

"When you landed in Fairview," Stubbs said, as though reciting a memorized speech, "we got off on the wrong hoof, you and me. I was buffaloed by Sam Archer and J.D. Hayes. I admit that. Those gents have the power around here, and a long time ago I threw in with them. I figured that was how I'd make money, but I ended up losing everything. I got my ass whipped." Stubbs paused. "Anyhow, you asked me why I didn't leave Fairview, why I didn't cut my own trail. You said . . . 'What's stopping you?' . . . and I handed you a sob story. Well, I ain't proud of that, either. I've been thinking about what you said, thinking about it a lot. Last evening when you talked about your uncle getting kicked and how he was stove up with a busted leg, well, what I heard was opportunity knocking on my door."

Roy was uncertain what the man was driving at, but he stopped sawing and nodded as though he understood all of the implications of his speech.

"You said you needed a ranch hand for summer herding and fall roundup," Stubbs went on. "I'm hoping you can set aside hard feelings toward me. I'm a good worker, and I know more about horses and cattle than I ever wanted to. Mister Smith, I want that job."

Unprepared for a heartfelt apology, much less an appeal, Roy put the knife down. "George, there's no need to apologize. . . ."

The liveryman interrupted him, driving his recitation to the last word. "To sweeten the deal, I'm offering the use of my two horses, both harness-broke, for the Dunston. What do you say to that, Mister Smith?"

"Call me Roy," he answered.

Stubbs eyed him. "Well, Roy?"

Roy answered with a grin. "Well, George, you're hired."

Just as strangers rarely came to Fairview, few residents ever departed. Now townspeople gathered on the edge of the street to observe an uncommon event—one outsider and two local folks departing, for good.

They watched as Roy said his good byes to Bess and Jimmy. Across the street Martha tearfully parted with a sleepy-eyed Frankie, and down at the barn Stubbs shook hands with his checkers opponent of many years, Paul Scott. Jay Dean Hayes was nowhere in sight.

Roy thrust a boot in the stirrup and swung up. The chestnut pitched once and pranced down the deeply rutted street, tail up. Roy hauled back on the reins. The day was fresh, the air crisp, and the gelding seemed eager to put this place behind him, too.

Heading out of town, Stubbs drove the Dunston with Martha and the baby at his side. Roy cast a critical eye at the vehicle. Stubbs's brass-cornered steamer trunk was lashed to the back of the rig. So was the coffin. Martha's grip was shoved under the seat. Delicate in appearance, the Dunston was anything but fragile. With a sturdy undercarriage and heavy axles, it was built to go the distance.

To avoid eating dust, Roy led the way. He turned in the saddle for one last look back at the settlement. Folks were returning to their cabins. If Frankie had been correct in her assessment of life in Fairview, the rumor mill was already grinding away. That skinny chippie, Martha, is leaving town to have another baby out of wedlock. Who is the father this time—the stranger who calls himself Roy Smith, or the liveryman, George Stubbs? Or that old goat, Sam Archer?

Roy glanced at Martha. Eyes reddened, she sat erect with the quilt-wrapped baby in her arms. She did not look back.

Martha O'Meara peered straight ahead, gazing at the horizon with the intensity of a sailor on the mainmast watching for landfall. Her first sighting of Laramie came after thirteen days of travel, due south on a sea of sage and thin grass. She spotted the telltale smudge of wood and coal smoke in the sky.

A train whistle carried across the plain like a mournful call. Drawing closer, they saw the steam engine pull out of town. The train built speed, westbound, with black smoke billowing into the sky.

Roy turned in the saddle and looked at Martha. She smiled at him. No words were needed. Laramie, not just a name now, was a half mile away.

In town Roy was welcomed by shouts from Harvey Baker. The liveryman came sprinting out of his barn when he saw the Dunston. He slowed and circled the vehicle, arms outstretched as though ready to embrace the lacquered body and spoked wheels. He danced a jig, a broad smile lighting his bearded face.

"You done it, Smith!" he shouted. "Damned if you didn't! Now, where's my team of blacks?"

Roy dismounted. "Somebody put them down."

"Put them down!"

"One bullet through the head of each critter," Roy said.

"What!"

"I found the carcasses in a ravine," Roy said. He gestured to the makeshift coffin. "Along with the remains of John Nichols."

Shocked, Baker asked in a whisper: "Nichols? Shot, too?"

Roy nodded.

The liveryman swore again. "Why would anyone kill that man?" He shook his head in disbelief. "Or put down two good horses?"

"Wish I knew," Roy said.

"Isn't there any law up there?" Baker demanded.

"Just what the local folks hand out," Roy replied.

"Hell of a thing," Baker said.

Roy helped Martha and her baby down. He pulled out her grip under the tufted seat. Stubbs untied knots, loosened the ropes, and lifted out his trunk. All the while Baker stared at the coffin in the back of the carriage.

"I kind of figured something had happened to the gent," he said. "Me and Nichols, we talked some. He didn't strike me as a man who would steal a rig and team."

Roy said to Baker: "If I can borrow a pick and shovel, I'll take the remains out to the cemetery. After I talk to Missus Nichols, we can pass the hat to pay for a grave marker."

Baker nodded. "Reckon we oughta help out the widow, all right. Tools are in here." He turned and headed for the barn doors.

"I'll give you a hand, Roy," Stubbs said.

The liveryman halted suddenly. "Smith, I danged near forgot."

"Forgot what?"

"A gent's been hunting you," the liveryman said.

"Who?"

"Don't know his name," Baker replied. "Some gent with a bum leg. He came in on the train and asked for Royal Smith. I told him you'd be back in town one of these days."

*Uncle Ab*, Roy thought immediately. "Was he hurt?"

"Walks with a stiff leg," Baker answered, "and asks for Royal Smith. That's all I know about him."

"Did he use a crutch?" Roy asked.

Eyes narrowing, Baker shook his head as he thought about that. "Cane."

"A cane?" Roy asked in surprise. "Where is he now?"

"Last I heard," Baker replied, "he was down at the Crossroads Hotel. 'Send Royal Smith' was all he said."

Leaving Martha and Stubbs behind, Roy hurried along the boardwalk to the Crossroads. The four-story hotel loomed ahead, distinguished by its size and heavily draped windows. In the covered entry a low-slung landau waited. Roy had seen the place from a Union Pacific passenger coach, but had never come any closer than that.

The largest hotel in Laramie, and the finest, the Crossroads was an imposing structure of stone blocks and red brick trim. It provided accommodations for wealthy ranchers and visiting speculators. Money men came here seeking profits by investing in cattle, minerals, timber. Few cowhands had the price of admission.

Roy could not imagine why Ab had chosen the most expensive place in town. Maybe the rooming houses were full. And why was he using a cane instead of the crutch?

Roy feared Ab had injured himself again, that he had come here on the train, alone, to see the doctor. Or had the wound turned gangrenous? Dark thoughts crowded his mind, not only about his uncle's health, but about their ranches. Who was taking care of the critters and doing the chores—Anne and her children?

He hurried into the lobby of the Crossroads where Persian rugs silenced his footfalls. He glanced around at the opulence, noting the clawed feet of upholstered chairs and settees dug into the thick weave of the carpeting. Two dozen or so men in suits lounged in cushioned seats. Some nursed cigars. Others clenched meerschaum pipes in their teeth. All of them wore city shoes polished to a gleam and trousers pressed to a knife-sharp crease. A few held pear-shaped snifters, drinking while engaged in quiet conversations.

*Not the sort of place favored by Uncle Ab*, Roy thought. He crossed the paneled room, taking in the framed landscape paintings on the walls. At the desk, he was greeted by a clerk.

"Sir?"

The desk clerk wore a visor, and now he pushed it up on his forehead. Clean-shaven but for a pencil-thin mustache, his sandy hair was cropped short. With beady eyes, the effect made him resemble a lizard.

Roy said: "I'm looking for Mister Abner Smith."

The clerk studied him before lowering his gaze to the hotel register. He turned one page and then another. Shaking his head in a quick, lizard-like manner, he turned one more page and ran his finger down the inked entries. He cast a doubtful glance at Roy, clearly seeing a trail hand unworthy of his attention.

"We have no one registered by that name."

"I was told Mister Smith's staying here," Roy insisted. "He's been asking for me."

The clerk eyed him. "And what is your name, sir?"

"Smith, Roy Smith. Abner is my uncle."

"Mister Smith, if I hear of your uncle or anyone else asking for you, I will be sure to mention. . . ."

"Royal Smith?"

The voice came from behind him. It was not the voice of Uncle Abner. Roy turned. The man had spoken from an up-holstered armchair against the far wall. He leaned forward now. Favoring one leg, he pushed down on the arms, and stood, cane in hand. He was trim, well dressed in a navy blue suit, his gray mustache trimmed. The man grinned. Steadied by the cane, he crossed the room in a gait that swung one leg. "I suppose we've both aged a bit since that last day of the war, haven't we?"

Roy stared. He realized this man had a wooden leg, a clue to his identity. Even so, a long moment passed before recognition seeped into his mind. He had seen him before. He remembered that day well. He had ducked into the regimental headquarters tent of the 112th New York.

"Keller," Roy said. "Captain Keller."

"Plain old Mister these days, Royal," he answered as he extended his hand. "After the surrender I resigned my commission and went home to Albany." He added: "Call me Jake, if you will."

Roy shook his hand, now recalling John Nichols had mentioned interviewing Captain Jacob Keller while conducting his research. Still, he was baffled by the man's presence here, baffled and at once relieved his worst fears about Uncle Ab's condition were groundless. Convinced the gent with a bum leg asking for "Royal" had been his uncle, Roy had jumped to a wrong conclusion. The fact that Harvey Baker was not acquainted with Uncle Ab had not entered his mind. . . .

"What . . . ?" Roy stammered. "How?"

Keller chuckled. "What am I doing here? How did I find you?"

Roy nodded, feeling sheepish. "Yes, sir."

"I received a telegraphed message from Missus Anne Nichols," Keller explained. "I believe she is in dire straits, but do not know the nature of her troubles. She said her husband had found you, but provided no details. Her message was terse. She asked for money." Keller paused at that. "Anne Nichols is an impressive woman. For her to make such a request, well, she must be in trouble, deep trouble with nowhere to turn. I attempted to reply by wire. My messages went unanswered. I even sent one to you with instructions to post it on the message board in the train station. No answer there, either. Now I know why. You were not in town. But where is Missus Anne Nichols? And what has become of her children? I have lost sleep over this thing, Royal."

Keller drew a breath. "As it happened, I had some time on my hands, so I packed my valise and boarded westbound trains until I got here. I questioned the town marshal, but that tight-jawed lawman was no help. He threatened to arrest Missus Nichols. He claimed she had lied about her financial situation, and defrauded the town of Laramie. Apparently he loaned her enough cash to telegraph a message to me, and then she disappeared. That's the marshal's story."

Keller asked: "Royal, what can you tell me about her whereabouts?"

Dust flew when Roy slapped his hat against his trouser leg. He walked out of the Union Pacific depot. He slapped the brimmed hat on his leg again, harder, and more dust flew. He had just learned the next coach to Hat Creek departed Laramie in three days. Eager to return to the L-Bar-7, that was too long. Every minute would hang heavy while he waited.

Roy looked back toward the Crossroads Hotel. He had relieved Jake Keller's mind a bit by informing him Anne

Nichols and her two children were on his ranch across the line in Colorado. They were safe and sound, or at least he had no reason to believe otherwise. He would know for certain in three days. Three days and one long train ride.

"What in the world happened to her?" Keller had implored him. "And what happened to her husband?"

Roy had not replied immediately. Keller had no way of knowing the answers to those questions were long and tangled.

"Right now I'm facing a job at the cemetery," Roy finally said. "Can we talk later . . . this evening?"

"Fair enough," Keller agreed. He jerked his thumb toward the French doors of the hotel dining room. "Join me for supper."

"Yes, *sir!*" Eager for a meal that did not come out of a saddlebag, Roy answered in a tone of voice that mocked military protocol between an officer and an enlisted man.

The humor did not escape Keller. He waved a hand to dismiss a bad joke. "Enough of that . . . soldier."

Aided by George Stubbs, Roy dug the grave with a pick and shovel borrowed from Harvey Baker. By the light of the setting sun they lowered the coffin into it.

Both men wiped their brows as they stood over a mound of freshly turned soil. The cemetery marked the crest of a barren hill a mile outside of town. At this hour the air was still and hot. In bleak terrain, weathered grave markers cast long shadows.

Back in town, they returned the Dunston to Baker. Stubbs stayed at the livery, offering to help with evening chores. Roy looked for Martha but did not see her.

He washed up in the trough, running wet hands through his hair and splashing water over rough beard stubble on his jaw. The hour was too late for a shave and a trim, much less finding a back room with a hot bath for travelers. He brushed dust and slapped trail grime from his clothes as best he could.

On his way to the Crossroads Hotel he looked again for Martha O'Meara. Among the residents of Laramie, he did not see her on the boardwalks or in the alleyways. He walked a dozen blocks and made a loop around the business section, hoping to catch sight of her. He did not, and headed to the hotel.

Roy did not know exactly what he would say in answer to Keller's questions. He figured he would speak in general terms, describing Professor John Nichols's arrival on the ranch with his wife and children. He would explain the reason for the man coming all this way to interview him. Roy planned to tender an invitation to Keller to visit the L-Bar-7 on Hat Creek where Mrs. Anne Nichols waited. Beyond that, he did not know what he would say to the man.

In the elegant Crossroads dining room that night the wine flowed. One pointed question from the former captain led to another rapier-sharp query. Alcohol loosened Roy's tongue. Drink by drink, flute by flute, he revealed more than he had planned, recalling a tangle of memories, old and new.

Jake Keller not only asked insightful questions, he was a receptive listener. Like few others, this man understood the full context of an infantry scout's wartime experiences. In the end Roy held back nothing. He told Keller all of it, including details about Fairview and the Bar-A-Bar Ranch that he had recounted to no one else.

Roy discovered that he did not need to remind Keller of the day he had ducked into the tent to relay news of carnage in Fox Run, the horrific aftermath of a Reb artillery barrage. Captain Keller remembered all of it, recalling events as if they had transpired last week. Now he listened to Roy's account of a stolen Confederate treasure, the source of wealth used to finance a great ranch in the American West.

"If apprehended during the war," Keller said with a shake of his head, "those rogue generals would have been hanged. Both of them."

Roy's mind teemed with memories, from this moment in a fancy dining room to a windstorm breaking in forest treetops high overhead. A long silence followed, a certain quietude in a setting of sterling silverware, crystal goblets, and pressed white tablecloths with monogrammed napkins, white, too. The silence was broken only by murmured conversations from the other tables, subdued laughter, and the musical clink of a fork or knife on a porcelain plate.

Men of wealth chow down quiet-like, Roy noted, quieter than the saloon company he kept when not alone on his ranch.

Roy avoided touching the napkin on the left side of his dinner plate for fear of soiling clean fabric. Only when he saw Keller use his vigorously to rub his mustache did he pick up the napkin. Roy unfolded it with caution, examined it, and then wiped down his face with the motion of currycombing a bronc'. He set the napkin on the table. Eyeing it then, he reached out and turned the soiled side down.

Roy looked at Keller. "Hayes still believes federal marshals are coming after them."

Keller considered that. "Ironic, isn't it?"

Roy eyed him.

"A stolen fortune," Keller explained, "bought everything except the one we all strive for in this life . . . peace of mind."

A commotion from the lobby turned heads in the dining room. Roy heard the cries of a baby. He pushed the chair back and stood. He hurried out through the French doors before Keller got to his feet.

In the lobby Roy saw the lizard-faced desk clerk bent over

a figure huddled on the carpeted floor. A woman in red gingham sobbed. Wild-eyed with fear or anger, or both, she clutched a quilt-wrapped bundle to her breast.

"You'll have to leave," the clerk said to her. When she did not move, he said: "Get out of here."

Roy crossed the lobby in long strides. From a distance he saw a blackened eye and abrasions on the face of Martha O'Meara. He closed the distance, knowing Martha had either taken a spill or a beating. He shoved the clerk aside and knelt.

"Martha," he said, reaching out to her. "Martha."

She looked at him, vast relief flooding into teary eyes. The baby made soft sounds.

The desk clerk scowled at Roy. "Damn it, she's bleeding. Get her out of here, cow chaser. Get her out before she ruins the carpet. . . ."

Roy did not plan to punch him. In a motion seemingly beyond his control, his right fist drew back. He let go with a blow that struck the clerk squarely on his receding chin.

The slender man fell back, arms flung out as he sprawled on his back. Eyes blinking, he lay there, stunned.

Roy helped Martha sit up. "Are you hurt?"

She shook her head.

"Is the baby all right?" he asked.

She pulled the quilt open and looked at the infant. Drawing a ragged breath, she nodded.

"What happened?" Roy asked.

"A man in town, he . . . ," she stammered and started again. "A man in town, he hit me . . . pushed me down . . . kicked me. . . ."

The clerk raised up on his elbows. Staring at Roy, his face was contorted with rage. He turned to a bellhop, a young man hesitantly crossing the lobby toward them.

"Get Shores."

# Chapter Eleven

Roy helped Martha to her feet. Aware of silent onlookers from the dining room and half a dozen more men halted on the carpeted staircase across the way, he slipped an arm around her back. When he steadied her, she turned to him.

"Frankie, she was right," Martha said in a low tone of voice.

"About what?" Roy asked.

"You heard her," Martha said. "Don't you remember? Frankie, she said I couldn't make it in Laramie. Not on my own. Reckon she was right. I wasn't here but a few hours before some man, he tried to buy me for a whore. I told him no, and he done hit me. Shoved me to the ground and kicked me . . . called me a stinking bitch . . . left me there." She wept for a few moments. "I fought him off, but I was so afraid for the baby. All I could think about was finding you. I done heard the liveryman talking to you about the Crossroads Hotel. . . ." She bowed her head and repeated: "Should have listened to Frankie."

The clerk got to his feet, rubbing his jaw as he glowered at Roy. "I will have you arrested on the charge of assault."

Roy faced the man.

"Don't try to get away," the clerk said. "The town marshal's coming."

"I'm not going anywhere," Roy said. "Neither are you."

"What do you mean by that?" the clerk said.

Keller stepped between them. "What is your name?"

The clerk cast a look of uncertainty at him. "Why . . . why are you asking?"

"I intend to advise your employer to teach you some common manners," Keller replied. "This lady is injured. She is in need of a physician, not a lawman to fight your battles for you."

Roy saw Martha cast a fearful look at him. She whispered: "We'd better leave."

"Too late for that," the clerk said. "Marshal Shores is on his way. . . ."

Roy ignored him. He guided Martha toward the front entrance. Behind them, the clerk uttered protests. They were halfway across the lobby when the door swung open. Shores came in, hatless, hair disheveled, revolver in his waistband. Behind him, the bellhop slipped away and made a beeline for the desk.

"What's going on here?" Shores demanded.

"Marshal, this man assaulted me," the clerk said, pointing at Roy. "I have witnesses. Arrest him."

"I am a witness," Keller said, "and I can assure you Mister Smith was fully justified in his actions. . . ."

The clerk raised his voice and blurted accusations, drowning out Keller.

Looking weary and annoyed, Shores said: "I've heard all I need to."

The terse remark silenced both the clerk and Jake Keller. Shores motioned to Roy and Martha. "Step outside."

Roy accompanied Martha to the entrance. Keller came after them.

The clerk called out: "Watch out, Marshal! That cow chaser is armed with a gun!"

"Stick to your line of work," Shores said over his shoulder, "and I'll stick to mine."

"He assaulted me, Marshal! Arrest him! I have witnesses! Arrest him!"

With another beckoning gesture to Roy and Martha, the lawman moved to the doorway. They walked out, leaving the clerk's shouts reverberating through the lobby. Keller came out after them. He closed the door.

Outside by the landau, Shores turned to Martha. "Are you hurting, ma'am?"

She shook her head.

"What happened to you?" he asked.

The lawman listened to her account of a man bolting from night shadows between two buildings. He had knocked her to the ground and fled before she could get a good look at his face.

The lawman said: "Ma'am, do you know where he is or where he went?"

She shook her head.

"I have no way to locate him," Shores said. "Laramie's not a bad town. I've seen worse railroad towns. Even so, no lady should be alone here after dark." He asked: "Do you have family hereabouts?"

"No, sir."

"In Laramie vagrancy is against the law," he said. "If you have no place to stay for the night, I'll have to send you to the county poor farm."

"I'll look out for her," Roy said.

Shores turned to him. "Do you have a place for her to spend the night, Mister Smith?"

"I know of a boarding house down the street," Roy replied.

"Miss Ruby's place," Shores said, nodding. "All right. You are free to go."

Keller stepped forward. "Marshal, that desk clerk is bellowing to anyone who will listen. He says you will arrest and jail this man. He has no right to defame a good citizen with such claims."

"I can't stop that weasel from running his mouth," Shores said. "I reckon we all know he's not man enough to scrape manure off the boots of Mister Royal Smith."

Roy was surprised to hear him say that.

Shores turned to him. "Abner Smith said you scouted for Union infantry in the war. That true?"

Roy nodded.

"What regiment?"

"Too many to remember them all," Roy replied.

Shores studied him. "Any man who served as an advance scout is a hero in my book. Dangerous work, calling for courage and stealth in full measure."

"I can vouch for that," Keller said. "I was Royal's captain while he was assigned to the One Hundred and Twelfth New York."

Shores drew a deep breath to compose himself. "I reckon we all have a personal stake in this. My brother scouted for General Rosecrans in 'Sixty-Three. 'The door to hell opened, and Satan himself was there to greet us.' That's what veterans say about the battle at Stones River. Losses were heavy on both sides. . . ." His voice quavered. "My brother's buried down there, somewhere in Tennessee."

Roy gazed at him. Shores's pained expression was cast in the dim light of lamps in the Crossroads Hotel, tears shed after all these years.

Shores cleared his throat. He ran a hand through matted hair. "Now, if you folks will excuse me, I'll go back to bed."

Roy watched him stride away. The lawman's boots resounded on the planks of the boardwalk, a cadence fading into the night like a muted drumbeat.

★ ★ ★ ★ ★

Roy had never slept with a woman at his side before. He had offered to leave Martha with the baby, but she insisted they share the bed. He had earned that much comfort, she declared, after a long journey on horseback. Besides, this room was the last one available in Miss Ruby's boarding house, and at such a late hour perhaps it was the last one in Laramie. Martha would not send him away to camp beside some murky creek outside of town. After nursing and changing the baby, she stretched out on the bed and made room for him.

Roy blew out the lamp. Pulling off his boots, he undressed and climbed into the bed.

He lay awake in the dark room, thinking back over the day. It had been a long one, starting with his return to Laramie and the mistaken belief Uncle Abner was here. That led to the shock of an unexpected reunion with Captain Keller. At sundown Roy and Stubbs had lowered their homemade coffin into a grave, interring the remains of John Nichols in the cemetery. Then after a fine dinner in the Crossroads Hotel came a confrontation with that clerk in the lobby when Martha had come looking for him. . . .

Miss Ruby had remembered Roy from his stay here with Uncle Ab. Expressing concern over the blackened eye and an abrasion on Martha's cheek, she shot Roy a piercing look. "Wasn't your uncle injured, too?"

Martha assured her that Roy was not responsible for inflicting any of the injuries. She slipped her arm through Roy's, and let the proprietress assume they were a married couple with an infant.

Now Roy stretched sore muscles. He heard Martha's every breath and felt her every move, soft and warm as she was.

"Roy?"

Surprised she was still awake, he listened while she reiterated her regret over her decision to strike out on her own in Laramie. Her regret was deepened by the fact that she had endangered her baby when she had been jumped. Now she was left with nowhere to go, no one to help her, no means of returning to Fairview—just as Frankie had warned her.

Roy felt her body quake when she wept. Not knowing what to say or do, he reached out and touched her. She turned away from the baby sleeping on her side of the bed and came to him. They embraced. Roy held her until the baby fussed. Martha pulled away then, whispering her gratitude.

Awakened later in the night by the infant's cries, Roy knew their meaning all too well. Those cries signaled hunger. The baby would not be consoled until fed. Martha opened her gown, and dozed while nursing. Lulled by soft sounds, Roy slept then.

In the morning he eased out of the room, leaving Martha asleep in the bed. She lay with the baby secure in the crook of one arm.

Roy descended the stairs and went out to the boardwalk through the recessed entry. After waiting for a coach to pass, he crossed the street and walked three blocks to Harvey Baker's livery barn.

Roy discovered Baker did not enforce the rule common among liverymen, the horse-barn commandment George Stubbs had heeded when he operated the livery in Fairview. Roy reached this conclusion when he saw Stubbs come down a ladder bolted to the interior wall. He picked straw from his hair as he crossed the runway. Baker must have trusted Stubbs, Roy figured, trusted him completely, for the man clearly had spent the night in the haymow, a violation of the liveryman's commandment.

Startled when he saw Roy standing in the street side entrance to the barn, Stubbs said: "Damned if you don't have a way of appearing out of nowhere."

Roy figured Stubbs was recalling the night he had jammed the barrel of his Colt into the back of his neck.

Stubbs said now: "I owe you."

"Owe me," Roy said. "What for?"

"For prying me out of Fairview," he replied. "The first day I'm in Laramie, I'm offered a job. A good one, too. Seems Baker needs a hand running his livery business, and I fill the bill. So he says." He grinned. "I won't tell him different." Stubbs went on: "Don't you worry none, Roy. I've got my faults, but I'm a man of my word. I said I'd ride your L-Bar-Seven range, and I will. I'll work till you and your uncle run me off after fall roundup. Then I'll come back here and work for Baker. Next spring, we'll see how things stack up for the season. How about that?"

"Fair enough," Roy said.

He picked up saddlebags he had borrowed from Baker for his ride to Fairview. Opening the flaps, he pulled out wrinkled and dirty clothing crammed into the leather pouches. The smell was strong, as the saying went, strong enough to kill a bird in flight.

Dropping the reeking bundle off at the Laramie Laundry, he walked on to a red and white striped barber's pole he had spotted earlier. An hour later he emerged from the tonsorial parlor freshly shaved, bathed, and splashed with cologne. All he needed now were clean clothes. He slapped at his trousers and vigorously brushed his hands across his sweat-stained vest and shirt, with little effect. Respectability would have to wait another day when his clothing was laundered.

He returned to the room. Martha was not there. Outside, he heard water splashing. Feminine voices carried to him. He walked around the building and found Martha at a water pump in the alleyway.

Sleeves up and mud at her shoes, she bent over a washboard scrubbing diapers. Miss Ruby stood nearby, holding the baby. Martha had washed her own clothing, each garment hanging in the sun on a clothesline of cotton rope. She gestured to Roy.

"Take off them duds. I'll give 'em a scrub."

"I don't believe Laramie is ready for that," he said.

"Ready for what?"

"For me to walk around town naked," he said, and went on to tell her that he had just come from the laundry.

Roy observed her as she wrung out the last diaper, twisting the heavy cotton fabric with vigor before hanging it on the line. For a woman as thin as she was, she was strong. He figured she had not eaten last night or this morning.

"I'm hungry," he said. "Are you?"

Looking up from the washboard, she smiled. "I was born hungry."

"Down by the depot," Roy went on, "a café called Tie Hack serves up good food. The chow's a sight better than that saddlebag fare we scorched over campfires between here and Fairview."

Her smile fading, a troubled look crossed her face. She shook her head.

"Oh, you two go on," Miss Ruby said. She made a face at the infant. "I'll watch this sweet little fellow for a spell. I don't mind. Not one bit. You two go on."

When Martha hesitated, the proprietress waved a hand at her. "Go on, get a good breakfast. Take your time over coffee. Don't worry about the baby. Holding this little fellow will be my pleasure. Go on, now."

On their way to the street, Martha grasped Roy's arm and

stopped him. "Miss Ruby, she figures we need a little time together. But that ain't the reason for me hanging back."

"What is the reason?" Roy asked.

"I have three dollars to my name," she said. "You done bought every tin for us when we left Fairview, and last night you done paid for our room. I didn't say nothing, because I figured I'd get a job here in Laramie. Figured on paying you back." She drew a breath. "I've asked folks and I've talked to Miss Ruby. There's no jobs. No jobs for a woman here in Laramie except. . . ." Her voice trailed off.

Roy pushed his hat up on his forehead. "I have a notion about that."

"Notion," she repeated. "Such as what?"

"The notion of you working for my uncle on his Box R," he said. "He needs a hand."

She eyed him.

"Maybe you heard me talking to George Stubbs about Uncle Abner," Roy went on. "He got kicked by a horse. Leg's busted. Uses a crutch to get around." Roy paused when he saw a doubtful look cross her face. "I know you tended to one old man, and he took a belt to you. Martha, my uncle's a gentleman."

She smiled. "Knowing you, I figured that."


Roy drove the covered surrey, the same vehicle John Nichols had rented from the Hat Creek livery. It seemed like a long time ago, that sunny midday when Uncle Ab had brought John Nichols and his family to the home place. Roy thought about that as he held the lines now, mentally reviewing a myriad of events that had transpired since then.

He looked over his shoulder. They made a strange caravan, he thought, a surrey and two horsemen wending their way across cactus-studded prairie where lush grass marked the meandering bed of Hat Creek. At his side, Martha sat on the spring-mounted seat, baby cradled in her arms. She smiled at him after she pulled the quilt open just far enough to look at the small, round face.

Jake Keller and George Stubbs brought up the rear. They were mounted on Stubbs's two horses from the Fairview livery. Stubbs had been right. Both horses were not only broken to accept the harness, they were strong and responsive saddle mounts, too.

Privately Roy wondered if they actually belonged to Stubbs as he had claimed, or if he had appropriated them upon leaving Fairview as a way to thumb his nose at Sam Archer and J.D. Hayes. Two saddles, blankets, and bridles had been borrowed from Harvey Baker in Laramie. Roy knew that much. Their agreement was to send the gear back on the next northbound.

Roy peered ahead. In the distance cattle grazed peacefully. Pride soared through him when he realized the herd belonged to him. Presently he smelled wood smoke. When he crested the next knoll, his emotions surged again as the home place came into view. Ahead he saw his ranch house with a wisp of smoke trailing out of the chimney, his barn, cowshed, chicken coop, and other outbuildings. He felt a renewed sense of excitement, a sensation coursing through him as the horses splashed across Hat Creek.

The door to his house opened. Two children ran out. Crossing the porch, Henrietta and William shouted their greetings. They looked back and called for their mother.

"It's Mister Smith!"

"It's Mister Smith! Mother!"

"He's back! Mother, he's back!"

Henrietta and William halted on the edge of the porch. Behind them, Mrs. Anne Nichols stepped through the doorway. She paused there, one hand shielding her eyes from the glare of the sun.

Roy followed her gaze as she looked past the surrey at the two horsemen, and then back at him. Their eyes met. In that moment Roy believed she divined the truth. Before introductions were made, Henrietta and William demanded to know if Roy had found their father.

"Where is he?"

"Did you find him?"

"Did you? Where is he?"

"Mister Smith, did you find him?"

Anne attempted to shush them. At once she stared at Roy. She searched his face for a signal, a hint to tell her that her instincts were all wrong, her worst fears unjustified. Her lips drew into a thin line then, eyes downcast.

"Anne," Roy said, taking off his hat. "Anne . . . I need to talk to you."

Henrietta sobbed suddenly. "He died! Didn't he? Father died! Didn't he?"

"Is Father dead?" William cast a fretful look at his mother. "Is he? Is he?"

Roy knew better than to lie to children. Yet he did not know what to say. A single nod answered their urgent questions. Henrietta and William spun away. Arms outstretched, both children grasped their mother at her waist, both crying until their breath was gone.

Anne broke down and wept, too, hands pressed to her face, shoulders convulsing. Henrietta pulled away. The girl ran into the house, sobbing. William stayed with his mother.

Roy climbed out of the surrey. He helped Martha down. Moving past the team, he stepped up onto the porch. He stood at Anne's side for a long moment, and made an awkward move to place his arm around her shoulders. Head bowed, she turned and pulled away.

Roy watched her stride into the house with William clinging to her. He cast a helpless look back at Martha.

"By damn, Royal, when you left here a hundred years ago, there was just the two of us. Now look what the hell you done. There's six . . . seven, counting that baby. What do you aim to do? Start up a town?"

Roy gazed at his uncle. Ab sat on the bench seat of his buckboard wagon, crutch at his side.

Deadpan, Roy replied: "I figure we ought to name the place."

"Name it what?"

"West Waterville."

Ab turned his head and spat. "That's no kind of a name. Call it Smith City. Call me mayor."

Roy grinned. Ab had been overjoyed to see him when he drove his buckboard to the L-Bar-7 from the Box R. Waving his hat, Ab let out a whoop and demanded to know where Roy had been hiding for the last hundred years. Then he listened intently while his nephew recounted events from the day he had left Laramie on the chestnut gelding to his return some four weeks later.

It was true. Their lives had changed immeasurably since the day Ab was kicked by a horse. Every day since then Roy had been eager to ride his range, rope mavericks cut from his herd, and stoke up a branding fire. Home at last was every bit as satisfying as he had imagined it would be when he had camped far from here.

He had been relieved to find everything in order on the home place. The next task was to locate cattle and make a count based on age and sex. Slicks would be branded. In the autumn tripled-wintered steers would be gathered and driven to the loading pens in Hat Creek.

With Stubbs's help, Roy got after the chores. He found him to be a hard worker and skilled, a man who did not need to be told what to do. Stubbs had taken to sleeping in the barn, a fact that did not escape Roy's notice.

"No smoking in there," Roy said to him with a grin.

Between the two of them, Roy figured they could handle chores on both ranches from this day through roundup. While it was true a rancher was never caught up on chores, much less ahead of the game, Roy took satisfaction in the effort and the progress they were making.

Uncle Ab had welcomed Martha's help on the Box R. Roy noted his uncle took to the baby right away, too. He had been a little concerned about asking him to take in the young woman and her child, but Ab had surprised him. Ab not only hit it off with Martha, he was content to mind the infant while she performed daily chores from sunup to sundown. Using scrap lumber, Ab fashioned a cradle and lined it with a blanket.

Roy slept in the barn himself for a time, giving Anne and her children solitude in his ranch house. The children ventured out to play. Roy noted Anne spent a great deal of time with Keller. Often indoors, sometimes they came out and sat on a bench on the porch, watching the children at play in Hat Creek.

Roy picked up enough of their conversations to know Keller was an answer to her prayers. A man of means, he had readily agreed to take her and the children back to Albany, New York with him. From the ranch, Keller would drive them to Hat Creek in the surrey. They would stay in the Plainsman until the next Union Pacific northbound steamed into the Hat Creek station. Then from Laramie, they would catch the next train to Cheyenne and points east.

Roy had seen lingering gazes between them. She was a grieving widow, and at home she would wear black. Even so, Roy wondered what else was in store for Anne Nichols upon her return to familiar ground in the company of Jacob Keller.

Anne came out of the house in the evening when Roy and Stubbs rode in. She lifted her hand in a beckoning gesture, and Roy touched fingertips to the brim of his hat. Dismounting, he handed the reins to Stubbs and went to the porch. Keller was down at the creek with the children, tossing sticks into shallow water and watching their pretend boats float away.

Anne said: "We'll leave in the morning."

"You can stay longer," Roy said.

She nodded once. "I know we can. Thank you. You have been so very good to me. And to the children. I wish there was something I could do to repay you. We'll always remember you, Roy . . . and what you've done for us."

They stood in silence. Roy found himself recalling the first time he had seen her. She sat in the surrey at her husband's side, her face and hands as white as chinaware. Now he noticed she was tanned from exposure to the sun, her hands darkened by stove soot. She stood erect, shoulders thrust back, gaze steady on him. She was robust in demeanor, strengthened from the relentless cycle of chores on the ranch.

She went on: "I will visit John's grave when we arrive in Laramie with Jacob . . . uh, Mister Keller. After we arrange for a burial plot back home, I'll send for his remains." She added: "Roy, tell me what happened."

When he did not reply immediately, she pressed him. "Please. I want to know everything. I feel I must know. You are the only person who can tell me."

Roy related all that had happened in Fairview and on the Bar-A-Bar Ranch. He meant to spare details of his discovery of the corpse, but she demanded every detail Roy could remember. When he told her, she wept. With sorrow came anger.

"A murder was committed in a wild land," she said. She wiped her eyes. "A murder was committed and the killer will never be caught, never punished. That is what you are telling me, isn't it?"

# Chapter Twelve

"Company, Roy."

Roy peered ahead as Stubbs pointed at the L-Bar-7 ranch house. It was Saturday noon, and he was expecting Uncle Ab. Instead of the familiar buckboard and team, a saddle horse was tied at the post. Drawing closer, Roy saw a gent sitting in a patch of shade cast by the porch overhang.

"Anybody you know?" Stubbs asked.

The man stood, hands on his hips. Hatless, he sported a walrus mustache, hair cropped short. He wore a black vest over a white shirt, and dark woolen trousers. Pinned on the lapel of the vest was a nickel-plated star within a circle.

"I don't know any United States marshals," Roy replied.

The lawman lifted his hand in greeting. Roy returned the gesture as he forded Hat Creek.

Halting near the porch, he took a second look at the saddle mount. The animal's left hip bore HC, the brand of the Hat Creek livery. A gun belt and holstered revolver were slung over his saddle, and a sweat-rimmed hat hung from the saddle horn.

Roy swung down. He handed the reins to Stubbs. Stubbs turned and headed for the horse barn with a glance back over his shoulder.

"Howdy, Marshal," Roy said, extending his hand.

"Royal Smith?" he asked, shaking hands.

Roy nodded. "I go by Roy."

"I'm Miles MacKensie," he said. "I came down from Wyoming to talk to you."

"What about?" Roy asked. He noted the bushy mustache somehow lent a mournful expression to the lawman's face.

"About Aaron P. Bowman and Jay Dean Hayes," he replied. "I understand you know them."

"Reckon I do," Roy answered. "Who sent you my way?"

"Lady by the name of Missus Anne Nichols," MacKensie replied. "She was backed up by Mister Jacob Keller, formerly captain of Union infantry. They arrived in Cheyenne by rail coach from Laramie, and came directly to the United States marshal's office. Missus Nichols reported the murder of her husband, John Nichols, up in Buffalo County. I understand you found the body." Eyeing Roy, MacKensie added: "I need more information. Missus Nichols told me about you. Both the lady and the captain spoke highly of you."

Roy jerked his thumb toward the door of the ranch house. "Come in. We can talk while I stoke the fire and fry up steaks for dinner. I'm expecting my uncle. He comes in from his ranch every other Saturday noon to pick up my list for the mercantile."

MacKensie looked past him, his gaze settling on the barn. "Who is the other gent?"

"George Stubbs," Roy replied. "He works for Uncle Ab and me. Come to think of it, you'll want to talk to George."

"How does he figure into the killing of John Nichols?" MacKensie asked.

"He hails from Fairview, Wyoming," Roy replied. "A few years back he sold his livery business to a rancher known in those parts as Sam Archer."

MacKensie said: "According to Missus Nichols, you discovered Archer's real name is Bowman."

"That's right."

Within the hour the rattle of a ranch wagon and orders sternly shouted at a team of horses signaled Ab's arrival. Roy stepped outside. The vehicle came to a halt. He watched his uncle use the crutch in a half-turn maneuver that kept the weight on his good leg as he got down from the wagon seat.

"Who's that, Royal?" Ab asked, looking past him.

Roy was aware the marshal stood in the doorway behind him. "Meet Miles MacKensie, United States Marshal."

Ab mounted the step and crossed the porch. He extended his hand and shook the lawman's hand. "As you can see, I'm slowed a mite by this-here crutch. Horse kicked me. Damned outlaw. I told my nephew to shoot the plug, but he won't do it."

MacKensie smiled.

Ab cast a blunt question at him. "What's your business here?"

After listening to the lawman's answer, Ab engaged him in conversation while Roy fried beefsteaks. Adding potato slices to grease popping in the skillet, he boiled carrots to round off the midday meal. Bread was included in the grocery list when he discovered the breadbox contained nothing but bread heels dried out as hard as boot heels. He went out to the porch and hollered at George Stubbs.

While eating the breadless meal, MacKensie posed questions and absorbed information from both Roy and Stubbs. As for himself, he admitted he was new on the job, having transferred to Cheyenne, Wyoming from Lincoln, Nebraska within the year. He had not traveled to Buffalo County, and had never heard of "Sam Archer".

Roy was surprised to learn, though, that the lawman had heard of Jay Dean Hayes. Following up on a request from Captain Keller, a search of federal marshal documents dating back to the war had turned up a file containing a warrant for his arrest. Citing "whereabouts unknown", Hayes was listed as a deserter.

Dinner was topped off by rye-spiked coffee. MacKensie leaned back with a hand-rolled cigarette, silent for a time. Until that moment, the conversation had been relaxed, almost casual. The tone changed in an instant when MacKensie's gaze swung to Roy.

"I shall require your assistance."

Roy stiffened.

"I appreciate your candor and your willingness to testify in federal court," MacKensie went on, "but I can see now that your assistance is crucial to the fair and just outcome of my investigation."

Ab's brow furrowed. "What do you mean by all them words?"

MacKensie drew on the cigarette and exhaled. "You believe the Nichols family deserves to see justice done, don't you?"

Ab asked: "What are you driving at, Marshal?"

"As I said, I need Roy's assistance."

Roy asked: "What kind?"

"Let me put it this way," MacKensie answered, turning to him. "You served as a scout for Union infantry regiments in the war. According to Captain Keller, formally of the One Hundred and Twelfth New York, your reputation is stellar."

"Hell, yes," Ab broke in. "There's none better than my nephew. If you don't believe me, go hunting with him sometime. Cougar or bear, you'll see. . . ."

"I heard enough from Captain Keller to know his credentials," MacKensie said. "Before I left my office, I ordered four marshals to meet me in Laramie, mounted, with a pack animal, panniers loaded. Soon as we join them, we'll make a hard ride to Buffalo County."

Roy stared across the rough pine table at him. All the

while, Stubbs had listened in silence, his gaze shifting from one man to the other.

Roy waved toward the door. "I was gone from the home place four weeks solid. I've got cattle running loose, horses unaccounted for, chores stacked up higher than a manure pile in a feedlot. . . ."

"Seems to me," MacKensie said with a nod at Stubbs, "this gentleman can handle routine tasks in your absence."

"Marshal," Roy said, "there is nothing routine when it comes to running a cattle ranch single-handed. . . ." He seized on an idea that came to him. "George knows Buffalo County and the folks up there better than I do . . . Bowman and Hayes included. Don't you, George?"

Stubbs acknowledged Roy's point with a shrug.

MacKensie dismissed it. His gaze was fixed on Roy. "You possess the knowledge and skills I'm looking for." The marshal went on: "The next northbound rolls out of the Hat Creek station tomorrow, noon. Be ready to board it. Bring your own weapon, ammunition, and personal gear. Saddle mount and food are provided."

"Hold on!" Ab blurted. "Hold on here! You cain't order a man off his home place and drag him to another state against his will! Not without arresting him . . . and you sure as hell got no cause to arrest Royal."

MacKensie extinguished the cigarette. "Sir, I can order your nephew to accompany me for the purpose of identifying wanted men. And I am."

"By what authority?" Ab demanded.

"Mister Smith," MacKensie said evenly, "I believe a war was fought over that issue."

Ab sputtered.

"The issue being," MacKensie went on, "the supremacy of the federal government . . . powers carved into our Constitution and inscribed in the blood of heroes."

The marshal's words were flowery and at once stern, leaving Ab with no comeback. Red-faced and jaw clenched, he listened as MacKensie continued.

"A federal marshal is empowered to cross state boundaries and make lawful arrests as required by the execution of a criminal investigation." MacKensie turned to Roy. "I don't take this authority lightly. Only after due consideration am I asking you to make such a sacrifice. I recognize you are a man who made many sacrifices during the war. Now in my capacity as United States marshal, I need your help in the investigation of a murder."

"Ever'thing you say sounds like a damned speech," Ab said.

MacKensie paused. "Here is a short one. Failure to comply is a federal offense."

Ab sputtered again, recovering long enough to fire a parting shot. "Reckon we could take this thing to court our ownselves, Royal. We'll just see if some federal judge orders you off your land after hearing you talk on the hardship of this thing."

Roy shook his head. He remembered the look on Anne's face when she had expressed her outrage that her husband's killer ran free, her disgust that a murderer would never be brought to justice. Roy had to admit MacKensie was right—she deserved to see justice done. So did the progeny of John Nichols.

Roy also remembered shotgun blasts in the dark of night, two loads of buckshot meant for him. At the time he had been intent on completing his search for Nichols. He was eager to leave Fairview, and returning to the L-Bar-7 had filled his mind. Now he acknowledged a larger truth.

"Reckon I have some unfinished business up in Buffalo

County," Roy allowed. "I'll ride with you."

Ab leaned closer. "You sure about this, Royal?"

"I'm sure."

MacKensie expressed his gratitude with a single nod, and continued the discussion at hand. "The Bar-A-Bar is a big spread, I hear, possibly the biggest in the state. How many riders are on the payroll?"

Roy shrugged. "I don't know."

"I don't, neither," Stubbs said when MacKensie looked at him.

"What's your best estimate?" the marshal asked.

Roy thought about that. "I didn't count the men riding in at the end of the day to stable their horses." He paused. "Fifteen, maybe twenty riders."

"Well armed?"

"I didn't notice," Roy said. "I know the foreman packs a revolver and a lever-action rifle. His *segundo* carries a handgun. Keeps a cut-down shotgun in his saddlebag, too."

"Why are you asking, Marshal?" Stubbs asked.

"I need some idea of what I'm up against," he replied. "If this rancher, Sam Archer, means to fend off nesters, he may have hired gunhands, a bunch of them. If I have to face a private army, I need to know that going in."

"Well, all I can tell you," Stubbs said, "is Bar-A-Bar hands ride into Fairview Saturday nights like other lonely cowhands from the ranches up there. They spend their money, raise a little hell, visit a crib, and ride out before dawn."

"I know who can answer your question," Roy said.

MacKensie turned to him. "Who?"

"Martha O'Meara," he replied.

Roy saw her crossing the weed-grown yard as she made her way toward the door to Uncle Ab's house. Martha wore a patched dress of gingham and a faded, threadbare sunbonnet. Wicker basket of eggs on her arm, she halted at the porch step, turning to observe two riders approaching. She waved when she recognized Roy.

The condition of the Box R ranch house was halfway between modest and run-down. The house and outbuildings were holdovers from the era of settlement immediately after the Civil War. A low structure, the pine logs of the main house had cracked and split open over the years. Gaps chinked with mud and straw. The wood had weathered to the pale gray color of a hive.

In idle moments Ab had threatened to knock down the old place. His daydreams featured a fine house of lumber and brick, real lath and plaster walls instead of shabby blankets hanging from the ceiling, and a shaded verandah outfitted with an upholstered rocking chair. The dream offered comfort for an aged man at the end of a long day in the saddle. But like other such topics of conversation between Roy and Ab, this one was regularly crowded off the wish list by the more pressing matters of survival.

"Martha," Roy said, "my saddle pard here is Miles MacKensie. He's a United States marshal."

"I seen that badge right off," she said. "Get down, gents. Get down and come in. I'll boil up some water for tea. I made biscuits this morning. Mister Abner Smith, he loves his biscuits, fresh baked and slathered with honey from the mercantile and butter churned from the milk of his cow." She repeated: "Come in."

MacKensie acknowledged the invitation, but sat his saddle. "Miss O'Meara, we cannot stay."

Martha eyed him. "How come?"

"We will catch the northbound tomorrow," he explained.

She turned to Roy. "You're taking orders from him?"

"Something like that," Roy said with a grin.

"Never seen you take orders from nobody," she said. "Except your uncle. This here marshal, he must have something on you. You under arrest?"

Still smiling, Roy shook his head. "We're riding to Fairview, and I figured you could. . . ."

"Fairview!" she broke in. "You're making a ride to Fairview? What for?"

"The marshal is investigating the murder of John Nichols," Roy replied. "I told him you might be able to help out."

"Me? How?"

"Ma'am," MacKensie said, "I understand you were employed on the Bar-A-Bar Ranch. You cleaned and cooked for Mister Archer, didn't you?"

"What if I did?"

"Tell me how many men ride for him."

Instead of answering the marshal's question, she looked at Roy.

"Tell him," Roy said.

"Why should I?"

Roy answered: "We aim to run the killer to ground."

She considered that answer. "So you're going after the killer of that city dude? You figure one of Mister Archer's riders done killed him?"

"We don't know," Roy answered, "but the marshal will be ready to make an arrest when we find out."

"All right, let me think," she said, her face screwing up as she mentally took a tally. "Fourteen, I'd say. Not counting the foreman and his *segundo*, fourteen cowhands bunk at the Bar-A-Bar Ranch."

"How are they armed?" MacKensie asked.

"Pistols," she answered. "Like most cowhands. Some own

a rifle." She thought about that and asked: "You expecting a fight, Marshal?"

"If Bar-A-Bar riders make a stand," he replied, "there will be a fight."

"They're cowhands," she said, "in the saddle from daybreak to dusk. The ramrod, Buck Brennan, he drives them hard. So does Mike Dwyer. Every day those men ride out. They move herds and tend livestock under a hot sun, in the saddle till sunset. The only gun play I ever heard tell was some shots fired at nesters, bullets fired high on purpose. Most cowhands, they ain't got nothing against folks trying to scratch out a living in this dry old prairie. Now, Buck Brennan and Mike Dwyer, they might. They just might."

"Might what?" MacKensie asked.

"Kill a man," she replied. "Roy, he knows. Don't you, Roy?"

Roy nodded. "I told the marshal about my run-in with Brennan and Dwyer. He knows about the cut-down shotgun Dwyer carries, too."

"I heard talk a time or two," Martha said.

"What kind of talk?" MacKensie asked.

"Mister Archer, he's bent on running off nesters. I heard him order Brennan and Dwyer to shoot two- and four-legged varmints. That's how he said it . . . varmints." She shrugged. "Reckon that's all I can tell you, Marshal. Don't know nothing else that would help you and Roy."

MacKensie touched a hand to his hat brim. "Miss O'Meara, you have been very helpful. . . ."

Martha interrupted him. "Sure you don't want a biscuit or two?"

"No, thank you, ma'am," MacKensie replied. "Like I said, we have a train to catch." He turned his horse and gestured for Roy to accompany him.

Roy drew back on the reins. Grabbing the horn, he dismounted. He looked across his saddle at MacKensie.

"You go ahead, Marshal."

Surprised, MacKensie was speechless for the moment.

"Backtrack to my place," Roy went on, "and follow Hat Creek to town. I'll meet you at the UP station in time to board that train tomorrow."

His authority challenged, MacKensie's eyes were fixed on Roy. Clearly he was deciding whether or not to countenance an act of insubordination, minor as this one was. The moment passed when the lawman nodded once. He must have weighed the consequences and reviewed all that he knew about Roy Smith for he abruptly reined the livery horse around and rode away at a canter.

Martha had observed this brief conflict between the two men, and now she laughed softly. "I didn't think you was taking orders from him, Roy."

"The biscuits did it," he said.

"Did what?"

"Gave me a bad craving," Roy said. "You got any butter and honey on the place?"

"Just like your uncle," Martha said, smiling. She looked over her shoulder when cries came from the house.

Roy said: "You're the one who takes orders. That baby hollers, and you jump."

She laughed again. "You're telling the bald truth."

Roy added: "He sounds healthy."

"Come in and see for yourself," Martha said. "While you're here, take a look at the cradle your Uncle Abner made for him."

Roy followed her into the house. *Ranch life has a way of making a man stronger if it don't kill him.* Roy remembered hearing his uncle make that statement over the years. He would change one word now. Ranch life makes a woman stronger. . . .

Roy had noticed that about Anne Nichols, and now he was aware of Martha O'Meara's swift stride as they entered the ranch house. More than physical strength, he thought, she was cheerful now, quick to laugh, and eager to tease. She had acquired an inner strength to match her outward, physical prowess.

"Life out here seems to suit you," Roy said.

"Better than I could ever have knowed," she said.

Roy watched her lift the baby out of the blanket-lined cradle, a simple box constructed from scrap lumber. "I believe he's grown since the last time I saw him."

"He's hungry all the time, I know that," Martha said. "Abner, he's making rockers so we can rock this child to sleep." She paused. "Roy?"

"Yeah?"

"You done told me your Uncle Abner was a gentleman," she said. "You was telling me the truth, just like I knowed you was."

"How did you know?" he asked.

"You proved it when we slept in the same bed in Laramie," she said. "You was a gentleman then, and you still are. I know you'd never do me wrong, nor would nobody else in your family, neither."

After biscuits and freshly brewed coffee, he went outside and tended his horse. He found Ab's axe and split firewood. He came back to the house with an armload to find Martha preparing supper. He stayed for the meal, helped her clean dishes, and afterward he held the baby for a time.

They talked long into the evening. Subjects ranged from their upbringings, to wagon trains, to war. Roy found himself talking freely, and told her about the last day of the war when he had encountered a creature deep in a Virginia forest. He had not mentioned the sighting to anyone except Aaron P. Bowman and Jay Dean Hayes.

Martha listened intently. She accepted Roy's account without question, offering no theory about the identity of the creature.

"There's mysterious things a-plenty in this world," she said. "Strange things we don't know nothing about."

In gathering darkness a coyote yipped, quickly answered by another, and then a third. Roy took that as his signal to leave, and stood. He grabbed his hat and headed for the door.

Martha followed him out to the porch. They stopped there. He turned to her and tracked her gaze as she looked up. Stars were out. They stood close together. Neither of them spoke. A moment came when words were not needed. She moved into his arms. Their embrace was easy and natural, as comfortable as slipping a hand into a glove. She looked up at him.

Roy bent down and kissed her. His desire soared as he felt her soft and warm lips pressing against his own. He held her, at once amazed and struck by a strong sense of inevitability. He had not planned this, and in truth he had never kissed a woman before, yet this moment seemed ordained. He pulled back and gazed at her. She smiled.

Roy knew a boundary had been crossed. Never again a girl in his eyes, Martha was grown and filled with purpose now, a woman desirable, passionate, and strong. Roy found his voice.

"I don't want to leave you here alone."

She smiled. "No man ever worried about me before. You're a good man, Roy Smith, good and sweet as honey and butter. Reckon I'll worry about you riding to Fairview with them marshals. That will make us even."

He held her again, felt her arms around him, her body pressing against his, and then they parted. He left the porch and strode to the barn. When he brought his horse around, he saw Martha still on the porch, a slender figure backlighted by the glow from lamplight in the house.

"Roy?"

"Yeah?"

"Tell Frankie she was wrong."

"About what?"

"Everything."

# Chapter Thirteen

During the war George Armstrong Custer was "Old Iron Butt" to the men of his command. The appellation was well earned, Roy had been told, given his proclivity for long cavalry marches to force the issue and engage an elusive enemy with a frontal charge. Years later, in the West, a headlong drive against another enemy would be the death of him and the bluecoat soldiers he led. At a place in Montana called Little Bighorn, he caught up with bands of warriors who stood their ground.

When it came to the capacity for sitting a saddle, Roy figured Miles MacKensie was cut from the same cloth. The marshal had said they would make a hard ride from Laramie to Fairview, and he had not exaggerated. He led them from dawn to dark with precious few rest stops. Even with a pack animal in tow, he shaved two days off the trek.

On the horizon ahead, a smudge of wood smoke in the sky marked the settlement of Fairview. MacKensie lifted a gloved hand and halted. Bunching, the others gathered around him.

Roy drew rein. He turned in the saddle, looking on as MacKensie addressed Leonard Reeder, Mitch Hancock, Simon Barr, and Lew Crandall. Like their leader, the deputy marshals wore a straw stockman's hat and a black vest over a white shirt. Armed with a .45-caliber Colt double-action revolver holstered on a cartridge belt, each man carried a Winchester repeater in a saddle scabbard.

Even though he had been at close quarters with them for seven days, Roy barely knew these men. Since leaving

Laramie, they had been occupied with breaking camp or making camp, tending animals and gear, sleeping, eating, riding. And riding some more, sore buttocks or not. Little time or energy was left for the camp tradition of swapping lies in the fire-lit night.

The deputy marshals exhibited a discipline the likes of which Roy had not seen among men since the war. Tight-lipped, they were bent on completing their mission, seasoned lawmen ready to take whatever action was required to bring in their prisoners. Quiet determination—that was Roy's assessment of them.

"Fall back, gentlemen," MacKensie said now. "We'll make camp and rest until daybreak." Backtracking half a mile, MacKensie dropped into a dry wash that cut away from the road two hundred yards. Out of sight there, the lawmen made a cold camp.

Under stars in a black sky MacKensie addressed the men again. "Mister Smith informed me A.P. Bowman is known in these parts under the alias of Sam Archer. A name makes no difference. Arrest warrants are in order, and we know who we are after. Mister Smith will identify Hayes and Bowman. As to the use of violent force, gentlemen, your judgment prevails. We did not come all this way to get cut to pieces, did we? Shoot first if some yahoo draws on you."

For the first time since leaving Laramie, the men were permitted to sleep past sunrise. Out of habit Roy awakened at dawn. Without a campfire to heat water for coffee, he drank from his canteen, sloshed water over his face, and reclined in soft sand while MacKensie paced. Watchful since daybreak, the marshal could not conceal his growing impatience. While he paced, he observed the brightening horizon to the east.

His plan was sound. Based on Roy's descriptions of Fairview and the layout of Bar-A-Bar Ranch headquarters,

MacKensie aimed to have Bowman and Hayes captured, in irons, and on the way to Laramie by sunset. From a lawman's perspective, it was not wise to tarry in a town where arrests had taken place and prisoners were in custody.

First, though, man and beast needed rest. MacKensie knew that. He waited as long as he could stand it. Sunup fired the eastern sky when he clapped his hands together.

"Roll out!"

MacKensie ordered the men to load up and mount up. Within half an hour they had eaten from tins in their haversacks, caught and saddled horses, and packed bedrolls. Mounting, all eyes turned to MacKensie as the men awaited his order.

Roy observed a silent, almost meditative moment pass between the marshal and his deputies. In that moment no one spoke. The men gazed at MacKensie as though manning a boat launched into an unknown sea. Released from safe harbor, all hands knew there was no turning back now.

MacKensie gestured to Roy. "Ride point, Mister Smith."

Roy spurred his horse and rode out of the wash onto the Fairview road. He looked ahead. Memories of the first time he had laid eyes on the settlement came to mind as he led MacKensie and the deputy marshals toward it. The familiar smudge of wood and coal smoke hung over the town where folks were performing morning chores or perhaps finishing breakfast. Far beyond Fairview the bright blue sky of morning shone above rugged peaks streaked by snow. This was, he thought, a "fair view" of a beautiful land.

Drumming hoof beats signaled approaching riders. The distinctive sounds did not go unnoticed. When the marshals swept into a main street deeply rutted by wagon wheels, the door to the mercantile opened.

Roy saw Paul Scott step out. Hesitating in the doorway, the shopkeeper ventured across the plank walk. He stood on the edge of it, watching armed riders angle toward the livery stable. Movement over there caught Roy's eye.

Jay Dean Hayes emerged from the barn. The fat man halted. He squinted at six horsemen, and drew back. Roy figured Hayes saw badges on their vests. He looked over his shoulder at MacKensie, and nodded once. MacKensie fed slack into the reins and rode past him, closing the distance.

"Jay Dean Hayes?"

Hayes looked up at the marshal in stoic silence.

MacKensie drew rein. He repeated his question.

Hayes looked past him, turning his gaze to Roy. "I believed all along you would bring federal marshals down on me . . . you denied it . . . denied it to my face . . . denied it in the name of honesty and truth. . . ."

MacKensie interrupted the tirade. "Mister Hayes, you are hereby ordered to submit to arrest. The charge against you is desertion from the United States Army. There is no statute of limitations for this offense, and as of now you are in my custody. By my lawful order, you will appear before a federal judge in Cheyenne. From there you will be remanded to the Commonwealth of Virginia."

"Turn that horse," Hayes said as though addressing a subordinate. "Turn your horse, and leave."

MacKensie signaled the two riders on his left. Leonard Reeder and Simon Barr dismounted.

"I said," Hayes repeated, voice rising, "leave!"

Barr drew his revolver, training it on Hayes as he advanced. Reeder brought wrist irons from panniers strapped to the back of the pack horse. When Hayes saw the hardware, he wheeled away. The fat man lumbered toward the open doors of the barn as though daring the marshals to gun him down.

MacKensie and Mitch Hancock hastily swung down from their saddles. Rushing after Hayes, they easily caught him. Each one grabbed an arm. In a brief tussle, Hayes was toppled. He went down with enough force to raise dust and knock the air out of him.

Mouth stretched open, Hayes struggled to inhale. He rolled onto his side, gasping like a fattened steer at the end of a lasso, a critter yanked off his hoofs and thrown to the ground, hard. Hatred filled his gaze when he glowered at Roy.

Drunk or sober, Roy thought, Jay Dean Hayes was a once-proud man. He remembered seeing him in the full regalia of a Union general on that last day of the war. Now the man lay sprawled in the dirt with lawmen standing over him.

The spill took the fight out of him. Hayes did not issue orders or resist when the marshals unceremoniously hauled him to his feet and placed him in irons.

By Fairview's standards, they drew quite a crowd. Bess and Jimmy came outdoors to observe the commotion. Residents hurried out of their cabins as word of a disturbance spread. Edging into the street, three dozen men, women, and children peered toward the livery barn, Frankie among them.

Watching the marshals, the townspeople saw Hayes placed under arrest and shackled. In whispers, they questioned one another, but no one could provide an explanation or a reason, not even Frankie. They noted a deputy marshal was left to stand guard over J.D. Hayes while the others mounted. Shod hoofs of their horses raised clouds of dust as they turned their mounts. The lawmen came down the street at a canter.

The collective gazes of the townspeople moved to the stranger named Roy Smith. They watched him touch spurs to his mount and lead the marshals out of town. Picking up speed on the northbound road, they departed at full gallop.

"Hell, I knew he was some kind of lawman," Frankie said, jabbing a gnarled index finger after Roy Smith. "I knew he was."

On Roy's recommendation, the marshals left their horses hobbled near the brook he had found in high grass. MacKensie ordered him to stay there and tend the horses. As a civilian, Roy was not to be endangered during the arrest and capture of a wanted man.

Roy watched the men depart on foot. He waited a quarter of an hour before violating MacKensie's order. Jogging to the overlook, he ascended it and belly-crawled to the crest. Inching closer, his field of view took in the back of the white ranch house. He saw the closed door to the root cellar, and beyond the corrals he looked at the cook shack, sheds, and outbuildings in the distance. The main horse corral was empty this time of day, as he had expected.

Roy watched MacKensie lead his men on foot to the ranch buildings. Guns drawn, they moved swiftly. Roy watched them shove doors open and signal one another with the wave of an arm. The deputies quickly determined the ranch house, bunkhouse, and other buildings were unoccupied. All but one.

Unaware of the marshals' presence, Cookie stepped out of his shack, carrying a bucket. A short distance away from the door, he swung it in an underhand motion, splashing murky dishwater on the ground. Turning, the ranch cook was startled when confronted by two deputy marshals.

Roy watched them shove Cookie back into his domain. The plan called for him to prepare a hot meal for the marshals, and then serve supper to Bar-A-Bar ranch hands as usual. The riders would be confined to the mess hall while

A.P. Bowman was arrested at the ranch house. For now, Cookie was instructed to do his work and keep his mouth shut.

The sun was low in the western sky when Bar-A-Bar hands straggled in. Surprise was complete. Disarmed and escorted into the mess hall, none offered resistance. So it went with the others. The ranch hands surrendered weapons in exchange for a plate of hot food, a tin cup, and utensils.

Roy eased back from the granite formation when he heard hoof beats. Raising his head, he looked to his left. Three riders came in, descending the slope that overlooked the ranch headquarters.

Flanked by Brennan and Dwyer, the man known in these parts as Sam Archer headed to the tie rail in front of the great house. They moved out of Roy's line of vision. Moments later came gunshots, the staccato reports of revolvers drowned out by one thunderous blast from a shotgun, and then a second blast.

Roy put down the Winchester. He scrambled to his feet and vaulted over the stone outcropping. Jumping and sliding, he made his way down the steep slope to the bottom without falling on his face.

Drawing his Colt, he hurried past the door to the root cellar, halting when the back door to the house swung open. Two men staggered out, both bleeding from gunshot wounds.

Roy recognized Brennan and Dwyer. He saw Brennan thumb fresh rounds into the cylinder of his revolver, at once looking back to see if marshals were in pursuit from inside the house. Dwyer broke open his cut-down shotgun, fumbled with one shell and then another. In the next instant, both men spotted Roy.

Brennan swiftly raised his revolver. He snapped off a shot.

The bullet went wide, but a second one plowed a furrow of dirt at Roy's feet.

Roy drew aim. With Brennan in his sights, he squeezed the trigger. The revolver bucked in his hand.

The heavy bullet shook the foreman and drove him back. He staggered in awkward, flat-footed steps while staring at Roy, his face contorted by pain and sheer disbelief. The gun fell from his grasp. Knees buckling, he went down.

Roy heard the shotgun snapped shut and hammers cocked. By instinct, he dropped and rolled. The first blast from the scatter-gun missed him, but the second discharge sent a burning sensation through his left shoulder and upper chest.

Roy planted his right elbow on the ground and methodically drew aim. Dwyer was in his sights when he pulled the trigger. The bullet caught him high in the chest, dead center. At this range, the impact of the .45 slug nearly lifted him off his feet. Arms flailing and legs kicking like a marionette gone mad, he went down, still clutching the shotgun.

Roy stood. Gun ready, he approached Dwyer. He saw the man's eyes blinking. Kneeling beside him, he pulled the shotgun from his hands. Dwyer struggled to speak.

"I ain't . . . ain't gonna make it . . . am I?"

Roy saw dark-red blood seeping into the fabric of his shirt front. This was not the time to lie to a man. He shook his head.

Dwyer blinked as he looked upward into the fading blue sky. "Buck . . . Buck's dead, ain't he?"

Roy nodded again. He leaned closer. "Who ordered you to dry-gulch John Nichols?"

Dwyer did not reply. Roy repeated his question, louder. He figured Dwyer could not or would not answer, but then the man drew a ragged breath and uttered a name.

"Archer."

Roy said: "Sam Archer ordered you to kill Nichols?"

Dwyer inhaled again, his voice weakening. "Archer said . . . said he'd lose the ranch . . . said we stood to inherit the place . . . if . . . if we took care of Nichols. . . ."

Roy said: "Then Archer sent you to kill me. Didn't he?"

"You . . . throwed a scare into him," Dwyer said. "He figured . . . figured you was a lawman. . . ."

A shadow stole over them. Roy looked up. MacKensie stood with his back to the evening sky, revolver in his hand. Blood soaked a shirt sleeve. The silence between them was broken by a gurgling sound in Dwyer's throat. Roy looked at him. He saw a beard-stubbled face stilled, eyes closed as though in sleep.

Roy got to his feet. He turned to MacKensie. The marshal continued gazing down at the bodies of Dwyer and Brennan. The two men lay where they had fallen a dozen paces away from one another.

"They fought like hell," MacKensie said. He turned to Roy. "You disobeyed my order. I told you to stay with the horses."

Roy eyed him.

"If this pair had not run up against you," MacKensie said, "they'd have climbed that slope and found the horses. We'd have been set afoot." He added with the hint of a smile: "Reckon I should be taking orders from you."

Roy grinned.

MacKensie cast a critical look at him. "You caught some buckshot."

Roy had forgotten about the burning sensation in his shoulder. He looked down at a shirt front peppered with tiny holes. He pulled the shirt open. His skin oozed pinpoints of blood in a dozen shallow wounds.

"I'll live," Roy said. He turned toward the rear entrance of the ranch house. "Bowman?"

"Dead," MacKensie replied. "I don't know who got him. Lead was flying." He moved to the shotgun, drew his boot back, and kicked it. "That damned greener sprayed buckshot all over hell. Two of my deputies are hurt." He swore.

After burying the bodies of Aaron P. Bowman, Buck Brennan, and Mike Dwyer, MacKensie gathered the ranch hands in the bunkhouse. They were a solemn bunch, having witnessed a shoot-out from a distance, and then venturing into the ranch house where hired hands had never been allowed before. Blood splattered on the walls and shell casings scattered across the floor were impressive sights. So were bullet holes in the portico outside and white plaster walls inside.

To set the record straight, MacKensie recounted in some detail events that had led to a fierce shoot-out in the ranch house. Then he changed the subject.

"Any man here may pick up his time," he said. "Collect your back pay, gents, and ride out after breakfast. For those of you who want to stay on, you will work as usual, you will be fed as usual, and you will be paid as usual."

MacKensie paused as he looked into quiet, sober faces. After a silence, the marshal answered their unspoken question.

"How long, I don't know," he said. "Probably through fall roundup when Bar-A-Bar steers are shipped from the Laramie pens. In the meantime, two of my deputies will be in charge. Any man riding for the Bar-A-Bar will answer to them just as you answered to Buck Brennan and Mike Dwyer."

In Fairview that night Marshal Miles MacKensie took

over the livery barn. By lantern light wounds were dressed, horses tended. MacKensie sent Leonard Reeder on a night ride to join Lew Crandall at the Bar-A-Bar headquarters. Both deputies had ranch backgrounds, both men fully capable of operating the Bar-A-Bar until the estate of "Sam Archer" was settled.

Locked in heavy wrist irons, Jay Dean Hayes was confined to the barn. Roy recalled their first meeting, facing one another in the threshold of this doorway. Sullen then and sullen now, Hayes was confined to the place, a prisoner not permitted to wander any farther away than the outhouse.

In rising anger, Hayes declared his innocence. He first demanded a bottle, then a drink. Refused, he looked on in seething anger while the deputies pulled a bottle of bourbon from a pannier, uncorked it, and passed it to everyone except him.

Ignored and denied, Hayes railed against his captors. "You have no cause to detain me. You have no proof I committed a crime of any sort." He shouted: "Turn me loose! Hear me? Turn me loose!"

Arm in a sling now, MacKensie came to him. "Mister Hayes, you will have your hearing in Cheyenne. The judge will weigh evidence and make a ruling. Until then, sir, suffer in silence. Suffer in silence, or I'll have you muzzled like a baying hound."

Hayes roundly cursed him, enraged until a visitor passed the pole corral and approached the barn door from the street. Wearing black from her high-button shoes to a long silken dress and a wide-brimmed black hat, Frankie appeared out of the night like a silent sorceress.

MacKensie crossed the runway and met her. She asked permission to speak to the prisoner. Perhaps she was a sorceress, Roy thought, for he was surprised when MacKensie granted the request.

Frankie entered the barn. She grasped the manacled hands of her old friend, and they spoke to one another in low tones for several minutes. Then she departed, head bowed as she hurried away in swift, bird-like strides. Even the iridescence of her dress by the light of lanterns suggested the plumage of a grackle. After she was gone, the marshal searched Hayes, patting him down until he was certain no weapon had been passed.

Sorceress?

Roy doubted Frankie was in possession of supernatural powers, but she may have sensed the prisoner's mad plan. He thought she was weeping when she walked out of the barn in her quick little strides, but he was not sure of that, either.

Roy knew the quart bottle lay uncorked and empty on the straw-strewn floor that night. He knew MacKensie and his deputies slept outside under the stars, all of them injured, their pain dulled by whiskey. Jay Dean Hayes was confined to the barn. Neither Roy nor anyone else knew until morning that Hayes had managed to climb the ladder to the mow. Even though bound by wrist and leg irons, Hayes crawled to the crossbeam. He pulled the rope to him, fit the noose around his neck, and leaped into darkness.

# Epilogue

As he had known at the time, Roy remembered the last day of the war, every detail etched vividly in his mind. He remembered the permeating scent of leaves rotting on the forest floor. He remembered the sound of a storm raging high overhead while he lay in stillness as though entombed. He remembered the forest creature darting away from him. He remembered the clandestine meeting of opposing generals. And he remembered eighty-four good men. . . .

Roy figured Jay Dean Hayes had been right about the creature. His explanation fit the circumstances. Not some forest fairy, not a legend come to life, but a cast-off from slaveholders. The creature was misshapen, Roy believed now, a human being surviving in the forest amid the goods and garb of fallen soldiers.

Roy remembered *West of the Moon*, too. Whether riding L-Bar-7 range under a pale day moon, or sitting with Martha on their verandah under a full moon bright in a starry sky, memories seeped into his mind. He thought about "love forever", the only legible part of the inscription, two words that gave meaning to his life now.

Married, Roy and Martha had five children in the space of seven years, two girls and three boys joining Sam in their family. Through correspondence Roy kept his family in Maine apprised of such developments. Over the years he received news from Albany, New York, too, from Mrs. Anne Keller.

In the weeks after departing Cheyenne with Jacob Keller,

Anne had been keen to learn the fates of her husband's murderers. Roy wrote to her in reply, informing her of the violent deaths of A.P. Bowman, Buck Brennan, and Mike Dwyer.

*High-minded thieves and their stolen riches,* she wrote back, her anger sharply slanting the letters of each word from her pen. *Thieves claiming a higher purpose! Still, they were lowly thieves!*

Anne was particularly upset by the suicide of Jay Dean Hayes. Both Bowman and Hayes had escaped trials by jury. *Fair and lawful proceedings should have been a matter of record,* she wrote, *with guilty verdicts known throughout the nation, history set right as John Nichols would have wished.*

*They escaped retribution,* she stated in her indignant missive, *and met their end in yet one more escape from justice.*

Roy did not tell her, but he believed she and her children had themselves escaped the recognition of truth—troubling as it was. Roy figured John Nichols had named a price for his silence, that he had cornered Bowman with demands for money. Roy believed he had been murdered for it. It was not a theory he offered to Anne.

For one thing, he did not have absolute proof. But he knew of a last will and testament signed by "Sam Archer". MacKensie had pulled it out of the rancher's safe with deeds, claims to water rights, and other documents. It was a moot point now, but the fact was "Sam Archer" did not exist. The will was a worthless piece of paper. Worthless as a will, perhaps, but with Brennan and Dwyer named as heirs to the Bar-A-Bar Ranch, Roy had no doubt Bowman had ordered the killing of John Nichols.

Did Hayes know? Was that why he chose suicide? Or did he expect to be hanged after a trial by jury? Roy would always wonder. He never raised those questions in his correspondence with Anne.

After fall roundup that year, the Bar-A-Bar was seized by the federal government. Broken into sections, the largest ranch in Wyoming was sold, livestock and equipment auctioned. Proceeds went to the government's "General Fund" to be dispersed later by Congressional decree.

General. When Roy heard that word used in connection with the Bar-A-Bar, the irony of it did not escape him.

A gray granite gravestone marked the final resting place of Abner Smith. At the crest of a rise overlooking Hat Creek and the south sector of the Box R, Ab had frequently paused here to point out the view from a swell in the Colorado prairie. Ab requested this "piece of heaven" for his final resting place.

Whenever the subject came up, Roy acknowledged his uncle's wish with a cursory nod. After all, they were busy day in and day out with the endless tasks of ranch life. Ab's leg had healed without complication, and, in Roy's mind, he was his old, bombastic self. The time for locating a gravesite lay far in the future. In truth, it came all too soon.

In accordance with Ab's wishes, the L-Bar-7 and Box R were combined into a single ranch under Roy's brand. Every spring thereafter Roy hired cowhands to tend the livestock, a few of whom had previously worked in Wyoming for "Sam Archer".

In bits and pieces, Roy told Martha about his service as an infantry scout in the Union Army. He started with the last day. Searching for the right words, he held her hand while he struggled to account for the strange forces that had swept over him. Looking back, he knew memories reached deeper than words, that memories haunted dreams. For him, the past was private, his alone, but no longer untold.